Blood Lake

C.M. Saunders

Copyright © 2025 by C.M. Saunders

All rights reserved.

No part of this publication may be reproduced, distributed, or transmitted in any form or by any means, including photocopying, recording, or other electronic or mechanical methods, without the prior written permission of the publisher, except as permitted by U.S. copyright law. For permission requests, contact Undertaker Books.

The story, all names, characters, and incidents portrayed in this production are fictitious. No identification with actual persons (living or deceased), places, buildings, and products is intended or should be inferred.

First edition 2025

For wandering souls everywhere.

BLOOD LAKE

–|–

Colorado, 1880

Dylan Decker had been riding for three days straight. He would stop to rest every four or five hours, sitting on the grass with his back against a tree and falling asleep for a while—more to give his horse, Skydance, a break than himself, though sitting in the saddle for so long was by no means a comfortable experience.

He didn't want to spend any more time in this part of the country than he had to. Ever since gold was discovered in the Colorado mountains, the area had been plagued by gangs of bandits, bushwhackers and assorted vagabonds. Dylan didn't have much in the way of possessions other than his rifle, some rudimentary supplies, and Skydance, but he was willing to die to protect what he did have. Most people would love to get their hands on a Morgan of Skydance's quality.

After an extended stint in sunny California, Dylan was making his way to his cousin's farm in Nebraska, where he had a few months' work lined up. The way things were going, he didn't think he would be able to relax until he got there. Or at least until he found a town with a hotel where he could lie down and lock the door. If his calculations were correct, he'd be entering Dudsville later that day, and if previous experience was anything to go by, small, secluded towns could be just as deadly as the open road.

The rough, pebble-strewn trail was flanked with tall trees and greenery. He took a deep breath, held it for a moment, and slowly let it out. The air tasted of pine, and snow-capped mountains surrounded him. Was that the last snow of winter? Or were the mountains so high the peaks were permanently white?

Where there were mountains there would be rivers and lakes. He could do with somewhere to water Skydance, just in case he didn't reach Dudsville by nightfall. Sleeping outside at night was one of the most dangerous things he could do. It wasn't just those bandits, bushwhackers, and assorted vagabonds he had to worry about, but after nightfall was when the country came to life. Mountain lions and coyotes were common. There were also three kinds of rattlesnake, all of which had the ability to kill a man. Even some spiders were venomous. What he was most worried about, however, were the grizzly bears that would be coming out of hibernation right around now, miserable, bad tempered, and ravenous. A decent-sized bear could tear a man to shreds without even trying.

Of course, he was equally likely to run into any of these creatures during the day, but at least in the day he'd be able to see them coming. If they came at night, they would be on him before he even knew what was happening, especially if he happened to be asleep at the time.

Dylan yawned and flexed his aching shoulders. He had to stay sharp. It would be all too easy to nod off for a couple seconds, slip out of his saddle, and fall to the ground. Six feet was a long way when a person wasn't expecting it. He might break a limb or knock himself out. Skydance, as good a horse as he was, would probably carry on walking until someone told him otherwise, leaving Dylan stranded and injured out here in the wilderness. That wouldn't do.

He blinked a few times to clear his vision, when he caught sight of something through a gap in the foliage where the trail wound around to the right. It was the merest flash of movement, but more than enough to put him on guard, because whatever he'd seen appeared to be coming right toward him.

Dylan's left hand tightened on Skydancer's reigns, while his right instinctively rested on the bone handle of his single-action Colt Peacemaker.

There was someone coming, alright. Maybe more than one person. In a world where there was little to separate friend from foe, and the terms were often interchangeable, it paid to be cautious even if it came off as aloof or aggressive. Dylan wasn't here to make friends.

As he and Skydance rounded the bend, they almost rode right into an empty wagon being pulled along at a leisurely pace by a tired-looking horse, and had to veer hard to the left to avoid a collision.

"Whoa, my Nelly," grumbled the grizzled driver, coming to a halt before bursting into a wheezy cackle. He was older than Dylan and clad in a tattered shirt that had once been white, but had long since degenerated into a grubby light brown with dark sweat patches under the arms. His chubby, stubbled cheeks were flushed red. All things considered, he looked friendly enough.

"Sorry, pard'ner!" he said. "Ain't seen another soul for hours and when I do I almost run him over. Ain't that the way? Hope y'ain't hurt."

"Nah, all's fine my friend. No harm done," Dylan replied, relaxing his grip on his revolver slightly when he realized the driver appeared to be alone. That wasn't to say he was, of course. This could still be an ambush.

"Good to hear. You look like you been ridin' for days."

"P'raps that's because I have," Dylan replied. "Just passing through on my way to Nebraska."

"That's a mighty long way away."

"Indeed it is. Would you happen to know of any lake or stream near here where I can go wash off?"

"Sure," said the wagon driver. "You just follow this trail 'til you come to a cattle path on your left. It'll take you right down to Blood Lake. Ain't that far."

"Why is it called Blood Lake?" Dylan asked.

"Because of all the dead Indians floatin' in it!"

Dylan's mouth dropped open. He was beginning to consider giving Blood Lake a miss, when the old man continued talking.

"Just joshin' with you, fella. It's called Blood Lake on account of all the silt bein' washed down from the mountains and buildin' up down there. Turns the water a funny color."

"In that case, I think I'll pay a visit," Dylan said, tipping his hat in thanks to the stranger. "Thanks for the help. You take care."

The jovial wagon driver was on the level, and a short time later Dylan was carefully steering Skydance down a steep slope into which a narrow, overgrown cattle trail had been etched, presumably by animals coming down off the mountain in search of a water source. The signs were good.

Presently, they burst through the last line of cover and were confronted with a shimmering expanse of unspoiled water. The lake, swollen by winter rain, must have been over a mile long and almost as wide. It was breathtaking. Staring out across the surface triggered some kind of optical illusion where, for a moment, it was virtually impossible for Dylan's tired eyes to make out where the lake ended and the blue, cloud-studded sky began. The sense of calm he felt was almost surreal.

Dismounting, Dylan led his horse to the water's edge so he could drink. On closer inspection he noticed that though the water itself appeared to be crystal clear, the rock-strewn shores of the lake were indeed stained with rusty brown mineral deposits, which in places took on a dull red hue.

Blood Lake.

Sinking to his haunches, he plunged his hands into the cold water, splashed some on his face, then filled his cupped hands and drank greedily, savoring the sensation of excess fluid running down his chin. This was as close as he'd been to gluttony since leaving California.

He instantly felt revitalized, and let his eyes roam the banks of the lake in search of signs of life. There were no buildings, not even a deserted fisherman's shack. Apart from Skydance and the birds swooping and cawing overhead, he appeared to be completely alone, which was just the way he liked it.

Strolling up to Skydance, Dylan untied his water bottles from the saddle. One of the first things he'd learned about the great outdoors was he should always fill up his water bottles when he had the opportunity, because he never knew when the next one would come along.

As he turned to head back to the water, something caught his eye. A dark, hulking shape was silhouetted against the shimmering blue of the lake a hundred yards away. He stopped and instinctively crouched.

They weren't alone after all.

He hoped what he was looking at was a bison, but in his heart he knew otherwise. He could tell by the animal's gait and posture that it was a grizzly. And a large one. If it stood upright on its hind legs, there was no doubt in Dylan's mind it would be over eight feet tall. What's more, it looked hungry enough to eat a man. Or a horse. Maybe even a man *and* a horse.

Time to leave, Dylan thought to himself. It would have been nice to rest up a little, but now he would be happy to sneak off without letting the bear know he was ever there.

Luckily, the animal had its back to him and there was a stiff crosswind, meaning it couldn't smell him. At least, not yet. The fact it was positioned on the other side of a leafy incline meant he was also sheltered from sight.

After another moment's consideration, though, Dylan realized he didn't feel like he was in any immediate danger. Instead, he found himself debating whether or not to take the bear down. One well-aimed shot might do it. Bears made good eating. It would certainly make a change from tinned beans. If he could smoke the meat, he probably wouldn't have to worry about food for two or three weeks. Plus, he could sell the pelt and whatever else he didn't need when he arrived in Dudsville for some spending money. He would be needing his Winchester, though. His Colt alone may not be enough to do the job.

Without taking his eyes off the bear, he began backtracking as quietly as he could, praying that the wind didn't choose that moment to change direction.

Luckily, the bear wasn't interested in him. It had its eye on something else. At first, Dylan couldn't see what that "something" might be. As long as it wasn't him or Skydance, he didn't really care.

Then he heard a noise. It sounded like a human shriek. At the same time, a figure rose from of the unevenly contoured bank and into view.

It was a kid. A boy. He must have been hiding. Whatever ruse he'd been trying to pull had failed, because he'd just been rumbled and was about to get himself eaten.

"So much for a restful time," Dylan whispered to himself.

Dylan whispered every swear word he knew, and that was one area where his vocabulary was especially strong. Now he had a choice to make. And the problem with having choices was there was always a chance of making the wrong one.

He could get back on his horse and ride away. Whatever mess the kid was in was a mess of his own making, and nothing good ever came from sticking his nose in other people's business, even when his intentions were good. Or he could risk his life trying to save a kid he didn't even know. Jesus, Dylan didn't even like kids. Too noisy and unruly. One fewer of them in the world wasn't such a bad proposition. It was survival of the fittest.

Ah, who was he trying to fool? If the kid died or got maimed as a result of Dylan's inaction, he would never forgive himself. He had to take control of the situation and use the element of surprise. No time to get his Winchester now. Damn it. And there would be no time to reload his Peacemaker, so he had to make every bullet count.

Drawing it to feel the reassuring weight in his hand and pulling back the hammer with a well-practiced thumb, Dylan edged closer to the natural curve in the shoreline that had been shielding him. He could hear the kid coming closer, running full pelt, pursued by the bear. The kid was mumbling something about his mother, the words falling from his mouth in a torrent. Dylan guessed his mother wasn't around. Any moment now, either the kid or the bear would notice Dylan or Skydance and from that point on there would be no turning back.

As Dylan was trying to think of a plan, the kid ran past him. True enough, his pace wavered when he glanced to his left and saw Skydance. He was probably more taken with the saddle and long holster than he was with the horse himself, because that would mean the horse wasn't wild and there were people nearby. Whatever the reason, the sight was enough to make the kid trip over his own feet and fall head first in the maroon dirt.

Skydance either didn't notice anything amiss or didn't care, even when the gigantic bear passed within thirty feet of him. He still had his long brown snout nostril deep in the water. That made him either very naïve with a dash of stupid, or very brave with a dash of reckless. This wasn't the first time something like this had happened, and Dylan was never quite sure which it was. But right at that moment, he thought Skydance was just about the coolest horse in the world and hoped he stayed that way a little longer.

There was the bear. With its low center of gravity and long, loping strides, it quickly closed the distance on the kid, who was now shakily getting back to his feet and throwing confused looks at Skydance, as if expecting the horse to rear up on his hind legs and scare off the attacker. The poor kid obviously didn't know that Skydance just couldn't be bothered with that kind of drama.

Shit. The bear was even bigger close up than it had seemed from a distance. Though when he thought about it, that struck Dylan as pretty damned obvious. Had he been expecting it to shrink?

"Just get outta there, kid!" Dylan yelled.

The moment he made his presence known, three things happened at once. Firstly, the bear stopped in its tracks and looked around quizzically, wondering where the noise had come from. Secondly, and making a mockery of Dylan's perception of children, the boy actually did what he was told, put his head down, and took off running along the lake's shore. Thirdly, Skydance finally looked up and became aware for the first time of the situation brewing behind his back.

Dylan knew he had to act fast. The bear hadn't yet spotted him crouching in the undergrowth, but it wouldn't be presenting a still target for long.

Using his left hand to steady his other wrist, Dylan aimed his revolver carefully at center mass, the animal's chest. That's where all the major organs were and all a bullet had to do was graze the heart or lungs. A lot of people might go for the head in that situation. The glory shot. Maybe saying "a lot" would be stretching it, because most of them died young.

Dylan had learned that shooting an animal, whether it be a bear or a squirrel, wasn't much different from shooting a man, and involved many of the same principles. He generally didn't aim for the head, reason being that it was a very small target. Even if he managed to hit it, the thing was made from solid bone. He could get lucky and strike an eye, or go through the temple, but more than likely his bullet would either lodge in the skull or simply bounce off. At the very worst it would take out the jaw or something else non-fatal.

Then, one of two things would happen. If whatever he shot in the head was prey, it would escape and, being unable to feed, slowly starve to death in agony. On the other hand, if it was capable of attacking in any way, shape, or form, it probably would. If he was in a gunfight, the pause between shots would give Dylan's adversary time to line up a shot of his own. Then Dylan would have to re-cock, aim, and fire again, but this time either at a moving target or someone already pulling a trigger.

In every conceivable scenario, the first shot was critical.

People often told new shooters to hold their breath when they pulled the trigger. That was horseshit, and fallacies like that were just something else that'd get a person killed quicker. What a shooter needed to do was fire after they'd exhaled and their lungs were empty. The trick was to be in such control of their breathing that they might as well be holding their breath, only without the pressure of knowing they were going to start turning blue in about fifteen seconds.

Doing his best to manage both his breathing and his heart rate, Dylan went through his usual pre-firefight mental checklist. Were there any other possible threats? Any possible accidental victims? And where would the bullet be going if he missed?

It was so deeply ingrained in him that it all came naturally, like muscle reflex. He didn't even have to consciously think about it. Though in reality the process might take three seconds or less, time slowed to an impossible crawl as Dylan drank in the sight of his adversary. It was an old bear with patchy, worn fur. And it looked like it'd been in some kind of scrap recently, as there was blood on its nose.

Unless that was the blood of the kid's folks smeared all over it.

Jesus, don't say that, he told the darker side of his mind as the finger caressing the Colt's steel trigger slowly tensed. That was one conversation he didn't want to have.

BOOM!

An explosion erupted out of the end of Dylan's gun, shattering the stillness and echoing through the valley. The gun felt like a living thing, almost leaping out of his hands.

Alarmed, or just because he was a miserable old bastard, Skydance nearly jumped out of his skin and let out a disgruntled snort. Dylan couldn't help wondering why he was so agitated; he should have been used to gunfire. For one horrible moment he thought he'd accidentally shot his own horse. Then, a fraction of a second later, the bear also reacted.

For all his good intentions, Dylan's aim was off and his shot went high, taking one of the bear's ears on the way. The thick husk of skin came away easily under the weight of the spinning .44, and was closely followed by a thin spray of crimson. The bear roared in fury, then reared up and started waving its arms around and shaking its head from side to side, sending little globs of spit and blood in all directions.

Dylan saw his opportunity and ran right past it while the bear was distracted, firing another shot at the thrashing beast to distract it and make sure it kept its distance.

Hopping on Skydance and settling into the saddle, Dylan gave the steed a quick pat on the neck as a "thank you" for his patience, then dug in his heels, literally spurring his horse into action. He felt a surge of power flow through his hands as he gripped the reigns, squeezed his thighs together and the horse began to run.

There was the boy a hundred feet away, still running as fast as his little legs could carry him. Good kid.

He was blessed with a shocking mop of bright red hair and skin so fair he would probably get sunburn from an oil lamp. As if getting chased by an angry bear wasn't enough to worry about.

Risking a look back, Dylan saw the bear was still too pissed off or disoriented to have started after them, and by the time it got its act together it'd never be able to catch them. It probably didn't have a clue what had happened, apart from the fact that its ear now hurt like a bastard.

Dylan steered Skydance to the right, leaned over, and scooped the boy up mid-stride. The action was so smooth that anyone watching it may have thought it was a rehearsed move. The truth was that Dylan was making this up as he went along.

For a moment, a look of absolute terror flashed over the kid's pale face. He looked directly up and started lashing out with his fists.

"Steady on, kid!" Dylan growled. "I'm trying to help. Work with me here!"

At the sound of his voice, the boy allowed himself to be hoisted up. Dylan plonked him on the saddle behind him and yelled, "Hold on!"

Just to be on the safe side, he dug his spurs in again and bowed his head against the wind as Skydance galloped along the lake shore. Where they went wasn't important. Anywhere else would do.

With something new to focus on, tiredness and lethargy were no longer issues for Dylan. Now he was motivated not to get torn apart by a vengeful bear.

The scenery flashed by in tranquil shades of blue and green, reminding him of one of those fancy watercolor paintings he'd seen at a museum in Ohio, and birds, spooked by this sudden turn of events, cackled and swooped all around them.

As they travelled, Dylan scanned the shore for possible escape routes from Blood Lake, which was certainly living up to its name, but nothing leaped out. All he could see were ranks of impenetrable foliage.

Just as Skydance was beginning to tire, Dylan spotted a winding path leading off the lake shore. He slowed the horse to a more sensible pace, realigned him, and minutes later they were back on what looked like the same track Dylan had recently left. It was almost as if the last few minutes had never happened.

Now that they had a little time to get to know each other, Dylan decided he should try to ascertain just who this kid was and what he'd gotten himself into. "You alright back there?"

"Yes," came the weak reply. "Thank you, mister. That bear was after me, it was."

"Sure was," Dylan replied. "What's your name?"

"Jerry."

"Nice to meet you, Jerry. I'm Dylan."

"Nice to meet you, too, sir."

"Okay, let's dispense with the bullshit flattery," Dylan said, suddenly unsure whether he should adopt a sterner approach when about to impart wisdom or take on more of a 'cool uncle' role. Social minefields like this terrified him. "What the heck are you doing out here by yourself. Don't you know how dangerous it can be?"

"I know, Mr. Dylan," the boy said, his voice cracking slightly. "That's why I'm alone, see. Our parents don't let us come out here on account of the Winged Terror, not even to go fishing or swimming, so me and my friends, we tell our folks we're going over each other's houses and we sneak up here to the lake. Today, I was supposed to meet Timmy Flip, but he didn't show. Prob'ly slept late, or his dad had him doing chores. So I came up by myself. Had to, really. We set a fish trap yesterday and someone had to check it."

"Fair enough," Dylan said with a smirk, remembering getting up to similar things in his own far-off childhood. There was also more than a touch of relief that he had escaped another potentially hairy situation unscathed. Then what the boy said registered. "Wait, your parents don't like you coming up here on account of the what?"

"The Winged Terror."

"What the heck is that?" Dylan replied. He was suddenly getting one of his bad feelings. The kind where he knew he stood on the brink of some revelation. He could quite easily walk away without knowing a single thing more about any kind of winged terror. It sounded like bad news. But that wasn't in his nature.

"You mean you don't know about it? Don't you have one where you're from?"

"No. And I wouldn't be askin' if I did. Should I know anything about it?"

"If'n you want to stay alive you should! Although it might not want to go for you. Too big. And you have guns."

"What are you talking about?"

"I'll tell ya if'n you promise not to tell my mom you found me up here at Blood Lake."

"Well, how about I just take you home and you can tell her whatever the heck you want? That ain't none of my beeswax."

"Deal."

"Good. So what about this Terrible Flyer."

"Winged Terror."

"Yeah, that."

"Well, we all grew up with it 'round here. I didn't even think there was anything unusual about it until I met you. I thought every place had one. It always comes this time of year. Spring. Though nobody really knows much about it. We don't know where it comes from or where it goes the rest of the year. It's mostly superstition and talk."

"What kind of talk?"

"Well, whenever a kid goes missing, even for a minute, all the family break into a panic and start yelling THE WINGED TERROR GOT 'EM! A'course, usually the kid turns up. But not always."

"What happens if they don't show up?"

"The Winged Terror happens to 'em. Swoops down like a giant bird or a bat, but part man, too. Grim sight it is. Black as night, and it has these massive wings, like thick leather. Big red eyes, too, that shine in the dark, and these awful long pointed teeth and claws."

"Jeez," whistled Dylan. "He sounds a right pleasure, for sure."

By now Dylan was half-convinced that the whole Winged Terror affair was just some fairy tale parents told their kids to keep them in line.

GO TOO FAR UP THAT ROAD AND THE WINGED TERROR WILL GET YOU!

God. It sounded horrific. It would definitely be enough to stop Dylan. And like the kid said, he had guns.

But now Dylan was hooked on the story and wanted to know more. "Have you ever seen it?"

"Nope. But I know some people who have."

"What did they see, exactly?"

"When you take me home you can ask one of them yourself."

"Who might that be?"

"My mom."

"Oh, really?" Dylan smiled, beginning to think this was all becoming just a bit too convenient.

"Yup, really. And she's married to my dad who's the town doctor, so she can't be altogether stupid."

"I guess not," Dylan admitted, now more anxious than ever to see how this might play out. Life was nothing if not an adventure. "How old are you, anyway?"

"Twelve."

"That's a terrible age."

"For who?"

"For anyone who knows you," Dylan said.

"Mister?"

"What."

"Did ya really shoot that bear?"

"Well, let's just say I shot at it. And prob'ly made it real angry, so tell your friends to be careful of a bear out here with a sore ear when they're out playing."

Dudsville was everything Dylan imagined it would be, and less. There was one main street with a saloon at one end and a whitewashed church with a clock tower at the other, the space in between the two landmarks filled with an assortment of brick and timber-fronted businesses and dwellings.

Dylan looked up at the clock tower, shielding his eyes with his palm, and noticed the tell-tale gleam of sunlight reflecting off metal. There was someone up there with a gun. A lookout. That wasn't unheard of; small towns often posted a deputy as an early-warning system, but usually only when they had an inkling there might be trouble. What trouble could a place this size be expecting?

As they clomped down the middle of the street, Dylan could feel watchful eyes on him. Being a stranger everywhere he went, he was used to that kind of treatment. A couple of times, passers-by waved, and Jerry would wave back or shout a greeting from his position behind Dylan. At least the boy seemed to be suffering no lasting effects from his close encounter with the enraged bear.

Only now was it beginning to dawn on Dylan how lucky they'd both been to escape Blood Lake in one piece. He could just as easily be delivering this kid to his mother in a saddle bag.

"Whereabouts do you live?" Dylan asked

"Here, here!" Jerry yelled, excitedly tapping Dylan on the back in case he had suddenly lost his hearing.

Dylan pulled Skydance to a stop outside a two-story building with DOCTOR'S SURGERY painted above the door and watched as his new friend slid out of the saddle and ducked inside the premises. He thought about going in to introduce himself, then decided against it. He didn't want to impose. Besides, he didn't know what yarn Jerry was spinning right now, and

Dylan was sure to drop the little scamp into a world of trouble if he went in there flapping his gums.

He was about to move on and look for a bed for the night when the door opened again and out rushed a tall, slim, outrageously beautiful woman with black hair tied up in a bun. She appeared to be in her late twenties, and was smoothing her hands on a cream-colored apron covering the front of a neat blue dress.

"Mr. Dylan?"

Dylan was momentarily dumbstruck. It wasn't often he ran into women this gorgeous, and it was even less common for them to know his name. She was so radiant she damn near took his breath away.

"That's me, ma'am."

"I'm Melinda. Jerry's mom. Melinda Johnson."

"Nice to meet you, Melinda Johnson," Dylan replied, reaching down and taking her delicate hand in his. The woman's skin was soft and tender.

"I believe I owe you a debt of gratitude," Melinda continued. "Jerry told me you shot a rattlesnake that had him cornered just inside the town limits. I do wish he'd stay where I can keep my eye on him. But he's so young and full of beans, he doesn't want to hang around with his ma all day. I s'pose I should be grateful he wasn't up horsing around at Blood Lake. If anything happened to him up there, nobody would be around to save him."

"It's no bother, ma'am, really. I'm glad to be of help."

A rattlesnake on the edge of town? That's what Jerry told his mother? It wasn't the most fantastical tale in the world, not like his Winged Terror story.

Dylan didn't ordinarily agree with lying and could rarely find an excuse for it. The world would be a much more bearable place if everybody just spoke the truth and let everyone else pick the bones out of it. But this wasn't his lie, it was Jerry's and if it made this fine woman's day pass a little easier he couldn't see any harm in it.

He had an idea Melinda sort of knew her little Jerry might not be telling the whole truth. Mothers always knew. Her going out of her way to mention the story was her way of corroborating it. And now that Dylan hadn't admitted the truth when given the chance, he was as deep into this as Jerry was. Damn kids, always making things complicated.

"I'm just cooking lunch," Melinda said, looking up at Dylan through a pair of deep, dark oval eyes. "We'd be honored if you'd join us."

"Thanks, ma'am. That's very kind of you, but I wouldn't want to upset your plans."

"Nonsense. Our plan was to have lunch, plain and simple. The more the merrier. I'm sure Jerry would appreciate it. Didn't you know, you're his new hero, Mr. Dylan."

"Ah, tomorrow it'll be someone else."

"Please?"

At that moment, Dylan caught a waft of something meaty cooking, and his mind was made up. "Well, since you put it like that, I'd be happy to join you."

He dismounted Skydance and used his reigns to tie him to a post outside. As he was finishing the knot, an older gentleman with a thick set of white whiskers strolled past with a cane in one hand and a dog on a leash in the other. The dog, a slow, lumbering chocolate brown Dachshund with floppy ears, stopped at Dylan's feet and gave one of his boots a sniff. Dylan's first instinct was to reach down and pet the tired old thing, but animals were unpredictable and could turn on someone in the blink of an eye. Just like people, some of the friendliest were also the most dangerous. So Dylan ignored the Dachshund and tipped his hat at the old man who glared back. It wasn't unusual to see people in small towns act that way toward strangers. Strangers often brought trouble with them. Or at the very least an element of the unknown that made folk uneasy. And this fella's dog being overfriendly probably didn't help matters. Dylan could see the betrayal in its owner's eyes.

The door to the doctor's surgery opened directly into a tiny waiting room, fitted with an old, scuffed three-person bench and a desk and chair in the corner. Knowing how most family businesses were run, Dylan guessed that desk was where the lovely Melinda spent her day when she wasn't cooking or seeing to her other chores. Make no mistake, it was tough for a young family trying to carve out a life for themselves on the frontier.

He noticed another door behind the desk, which must've led to the doctor's examination room. It was closed, but as they passed, a loud, gruff shout came from within, closely followed by a string of swear words.

Melinda must have noticed Dylan's unease, because as she waved him through and toward a sturdy-looking wooden staircase. "Don't be concerned about that," she said. "Old Lenny Hood fell off his horse and popped his knee out again. My husband is just fixing him up and will be joining us shortly. The surgery is always quiet in the afternoons. Apart from the time the Dolan brothers started a gunfight outside the saloon and five people got shot. That was a busy day indeed."

"I'm sure it was, ma'am."

The rooms above the shop were the Johnson family's living quarters, made up of a large kitchen and living area with several closed doors leading off it. Dylan guessed they were bedrooms. Here, the tantalizing aroma was almost dizzying and when he happened a glance at the stove, he saw a steaming pot almost overflowing with home-cooked goodness.

"Whatever that is, it smells delicious!" he said. And he wasn't just being polite. He'd spent more than enough nights eating vermin off campfires to appreciate a home-cooked meal. It was all he could do to refrain from cheering.

"Beef stew. My dear old grandmother's famous recipe. Well, famous in Dudsville, anyway. Sit, sit," Melinda said, pulling out a chair at the kitchen table bedecked with a flowery tablecloth. "I do hope that's okay for you."

"It's more than okay, ma'am. And very kind of you," Dylan said, taking his place at the table and casting his eyes around the simply furnished room. It was strange how he felt more out of place in a warm, homey environment like this than he did out in the wilderness with only Skydance and his thoughts for company.

He was soon joined at the table by Jerry, who he greeted with a wink. The boy smiled and went off to help his mother. Soon, there were four places set, and a large pot of stew with a plate of fresh baked rolls sitting in the middle of the table.

"Don't bother waiting for my husband, he'll be up when he's finished," said Melinda, sitting down at the table with no small measure of grace and elegance.

No sooner had the words left her mouth when there was a *clomp clomp clomp* on the wooden staircase. The door opened inward, and there stood a tall, lanky, clean-shaven fellow wearing spectacles. "Ah! You must be Mr. Dylan, the latest man to come to the aid of my tearaway offspring! Doctor Johnson, at your service!"

Dylan politely stood to greet the man and accepted his handshake, noting that his hand was almost as soft as his wife's. "It's just Dylan, and I think coming to the boy's aid is over-selling it a little. I'm sure he would've been fine had I not come riding up on him."

"Sure, fine with a leg full of rattler venom."

"Well, even if that did happen, at least he'd know where to come."

"I mostly treat cases of influenza, scurvy, and cholera," Doctor Johnson explained. "I do get to remove bullets or set broken bones from time to time, but rattlesnake bites are surprisingly rare. Most folk have the good sense to run when they come across one. Seems my boy didn't have that good sense. Knowing him, he poked it with a stick. I see you've already met my good wife?"

"I have indeed," Dylan replied, sitting back down, "And let me just say you are a very lucky man, if you didn't know it already."

"Oh, believe me, I am fully aware of that," the doctor said with an adoring glance at his wife as she blushed and stifled a girlish giggle with the back of her hand. "You wait 'til you taste her cooking."

Doctor Johnson wasn't exaggerating. The stew, succulent chunks of off-the-bone beef braised in spices with new potatoes, carrots, and beans, was delicious, and Dylan didn't hesitate for a moment when Melinda offered second helpings.

The conversation was light and good natured, with Dylan answering the usual array of getting-to-know-you questions as politely as he could and explaining he was passing through Dudsville on his way to pick up some work in Nebraska.

Despite the good company and better food, throughout the meal, one thing was at the forefront of Dylan's mind. The Winged Terror. He couldn't seem to shake it. More accurately, he couldn't shake the image Jerry had implanted in his mind. If he was making that up, the boy had a great career as a writer ahead of him.

As Dylan was wondering how he could deflect attention away from him and onto this make-believe monster, Jerry saved him the trouble.

"Mr. Dylan, I have a gun, too. Do you wanna see it? Pa says every kid in Dudsville should know how to shoot on account of the Winged Terror."

"Oh, I'm sure Mr. Dylan doesn't want to be bothered by you waving that old thing around," Melinda interjected.

"No, that's fine," Dylan said, wiping his mouth with a napkin as daintily as he could. "I would love to see it."

"Yes!" Jerry exclaimed, jumping off his chair and bounding across the room in the direction of one of the closed doors.

"The boy mentioned this Winged Terror before," Dylan said by way of testing the water. "It's some kind of local legend or folk tale, right?"

"Oh no, it's much more than that," Doctor Johnson said, without the trace of a smile. "The Winged Terror is real enough, and something we been dealing with for a long time around here."

"What is it, exactly?"

"Nobody really knows," Melinda said.

"It's the Winged Terror, that's what it is," Doctor Johnson insisted. "Some say it's a forgotten species, like some kind of dinosaur, others maintain it's some kind of demon, or the product of witchcraft. Some blamed the local Indian tribes, but they have their own stories about something similar going back thousands of years."

"Interesting," Dylan said, turning his gaze to Melinda. "Jerry told me you saw it once. Is that true?"

Melinda Johnson immediately cast her eyes down self-consciously and her right eyelid twitched. "It's true," she confessed. "Though I was barely Jerry's age at the time, I remember it as if it happened yesterday."

"Could it have been an eagle or some other bird or animal?" Dylan offered.

"Not unless eagles grow to be over eight feet tall. Trust me, Mr. Dylan, I was raised here. My pa hunted and trapped every kind of animal you can imagine. I know all the wildlife a person can reasonably expect to come across, and this wasn't any of those. It was something...else. Something evil."

The woman's tone convinced Dylan of her sincerity, and without any more prompting, she continued.

"Me and my sisters saw it circling above us while we were out playing near Blood Lake. Didn't take much notice at first, though now we think it was watching us, waiting for one of us to break away from the others so it could swoop down and take us. That's exactly what had happened with poor Johnny Sweetweather the spring before. His friend said both he and Johnny watched this thing in the sky for an age before it saw its opportunity."

"You saw it clearly?"

"As clearly as I'm seeing you now. It was eight feet tall, and with its wings spread out it was almost as wide. They made this awful, loud beating sound that got louder and louder as it came for us. Then I saw its eyes. Bright red, they were, as if they were...shining. But the thing I remember most is the smell. It stank like death, if Death happened to be wearing Jerry's sweaty socks. It was so strong it made our eyes water and my sister Tammy threw up her breakfast. We were lucky. The thing came down, and missed us by a feather's width. It didn't miss Johnny Sweetweather, though. It picked him up, carried him away, and nobody seen him since. His poor parents never did quite get over it. His pa drank himself into an early grave and his mom died a heartbroken widow. That's why we always tell our children to never go beyond the town limits on their own. A'course that's always assuming the thing won't dare come to town. It would if it got hungry enough."

"Why would this Winged Terror take children?" asked Dylan. Suddenly, his appetite was waning. Either that or the hole in his stomach had finally been filled.

"Because children are small enough to carry off," the doctor said with a shrug. And it's hungry."

"It eats them?"

"What else would it do?" Melinda replied. "It wasn't just Johnny Sweetweather. There have been dozens over the years, none of them ever heard from again. And it's not just children. A couple of adults have been taken over the years, older folk. Frail and weak. And scores of pets and other animals like sheep and chickens. Nothing too big. Let's just say a lot of animals go missing around here come spring time."

Melinda's eyelid twitched again. The smile had long since slipped, and the pained expression that replaced it belied a lifetime of angst. Dylan couldn't imagine living like this. Never able to relax, always watching the skies and constantly worrying about suddenly losing the thing she cared about most. She wasn't lying about seeing the beast. Either what she was saying was true, or she thought it was true. And if that were the case, she wasn't the only one who believed it. The whole town, or the whole family at least, must be under some kind of freaky shared delusion.

At that moment, Jerry appeared waving a small-caliber varmint rifle. The stock had been shortened to make it easier for the boy to handle, and though the weapon wasn't big enough to cause any real damage, it would be powerful enough to punch a hole in almost anything up to fifty or sixty yards.

"Don't you worry, Mom," Jerry said, in a calm, measured tone that belied his tender years. "If that Winged Terror ever comes near me, I'll shoot it right between the eyes."

"Might be better going for the actual eyes, rather than the bony place in between them," Dylan added helpfully.

"Thanks for the tip, Mr. Dylan. I wish I'd taken my rifle out with me this morning and shot that snake myself, but I didn't think I'd need to as I was only going to the end of the street."

"Sure, sure..."

"Besides, if I had taken it with me, I might never have met you and we wouldn't be here now."

"That's something, at least," Dylan said, trying to make himself appear more enthusiastic than he really was. "What else do you know about this Winged Terror?"

"Well, we know it comes out for only a couple of months each year, round about now," Doctor Johnson added. "Must be something to do with hibernation patterns or its feeding cycle or something. It's often seen in the skies; waiting, watching."

"Couldn't it just be eagles or vultures people are seeing up there?" Dylan wondered aloud, still not entirely convinced.

"Maybe some," the doctor replied. "But definitely not all. As a town, we group together to protect what's ours. We've learned to plan for it each year, so we build up our defenses, keep an eye on our kids and pets, and post lookouts."

"In the church clock tower, right?"

"That's one location. You can get a good view from there," Doctor Johnson said, standing and offering his hand to be shook once again. "I'd love to stay and talk about it some more, but I really should be getting back to work."

"Sure," Dylan replied. "No problem."

"I'd like to pay you back for the good turn you did my son."

"That's not necessary, really."

"No. I insist. Every good deed should be rewarded. I gather you've been on the road a while. You must be crying out for a soft bed. I have an arrangement with Von Williams, who runs the hotel here. Whenever out-of-town patients come in for appointments, I send them over to the Williams place and he gives them a discount on the rooms. Let me pay for a night for you, then you can be on your way, nice and refreshed, first thing in the morning."

That did sound like a good idea, and Dylan found it difficult to resist. Saying "no" had always been his problem. Or one of them.

"Maybe we can meet up again later, if you're feeling sociable," Doctor Johnson continued. "I'd be more than happy to buy you a drink. In the meantime, I'll see about getting this room arranged."

Dylan bid Melinda and Jerry goodbye, thanking the former once again for her kindness and reminding the latter to exercise some caution and common sense when out playing in future, and followed Doctor Johnson down the wooden staircase.

The street outside was relatively quiet for a sunny spring afternoon. As Dylan and Doctor Johnson walked with Dylan leading Skydance by his reigns, a few people passed them by, all of whom tipped their hat to the doctor and mumbled greetings.

A good barometer of a man's character is the way he is treated by people who know him, and in this case Dylan felt he was in safe hands. As a bonus he was popular by association, which made a pleasant change.

On the way to the hotel they passed several small businesses, including a post office and a barber shop, which Dylan earmarked for a visit before he left town. He couldn't remember the last time he'd had a shave and a haircut that didn't involve his Bowie knife.

Several times during the short journey, Dylan couldn't prevent his gaze being drawn to the heavens. The sky was clear, but he could imagine how it must feel to be a little kid looking up and seeing some giant bat-like creature straight out of their nightmares swooping down at them. If the stories about the Winged Terror were true, how much death and misery was it responsible for? It was high time someone evened the score.

About halfway along the street, Doctor Johnson, Dylan, and Skydance stopped outside a large, glass-fronted timber-framed building with a row of hitching posts outside. The three or four horses already tied to them suggested it was busy inside. As Dylan patted Skydance on the head and tied his reigns alongside the other horses, he chanced a quick glance through the window.

Doctor Johnson was already chatting with a skinny, nervous-looking fella behind the counter. Von Williams, the proprietor, he imagined. He wore a pair of round glasses and was balding on top.

The talk seemed to be going well. Some money changed hands; Dylan couldn't see how much, but it must be a pretty penny. This place looked fancy. No doubt it was a sporting house as well as a hotel, and might also be a front for any number of nefarious activities that were not his concern. It was unlikely that a town this size could support a place like this otherwise.

As long as nobody got hurt and whatever people did didn't infringe on him in any way, Dylan was happy to turn a blind eye.

Unbuckling his saddle, saddle bags, and rifle was always a chore, Dylan thought to himself as he methodically set about stripping down Skydance, the horse offering a tired snort by way of thanks. This stuff was unwieldy and heavy, which was exactly why a man employed an animal to carry it for him.

Now laden with gear, Dylan entered the hotel just as Doc Johnson was leaving.

"All settled," the doctor announced buoyantly. "Enjoy your stay. It's a nice place. And come along to the saloon tonight. I'll introduce you to the sheriff and buy you that drink I promised."

"That's very kind of you," Dylan replied, taken aback by the man's generosity. "Thanks for the room, and the invite. I might take you up on that drink."

"Welcome," the doctor said with a wave. "I have to be getting back to work, Mr. Dylan. It's been a pleasure. Hope to see you again."

And then he was gone. That last sentence was sincere. Dylan could hear it in the man's voice. More times than not he got a casual "see ya," and gave an equally flippant response, both parties knowing they probably wouldn't be seeing each other again and had no plans to go out of their way to do so. If a person was a drifter, like Dylan, the odds were that they were just passing through and their paths happened to intersect for a brief time before they both went their separate ways. Even if a person was the settled type with the same people around them day after day, as sad as it was, there would inevitably come a time when either one wouldn't be there.

The lobby of the hotel was plush. There were a lot of polished oak cabinets, leather wingback chairs, and soft furnishings. A huge, horned deer head was fixed to a wall above a bookshelf and the golden sunlight streaming through the windows made everything appear even more luxurious.

Before Dylan could fully absorb the new environment, the skinny, nervous-looking fella Doc Johnson had been talking to approached.

"Welcome, sir. Come this way, please. I'll show you to your room."

The room Dylan was on the ground floor. Another win. On another day, it might have been up three or four flights of stairs that he would have to navigate with his arms full of saddle bags and guns.

"Would you like me to prepare a bath for you, sir?"

"A bath?"

"Yes, sir."

"With hot water?"

"As hot as you can stand," said the man, who Dylan was now warming to in no uncertain terms. "Doc Johnson has paid for what we call our Gold Star package. That means you are permitted full use of all our facilities for not a minute less than a full twenty-four hours."

"Is that right? That's pretty nice of him."

"It is indeed, sir. We'll also put your horse in the stables out back. Yours is the fine-looking black Morgan with flecks of tan and the white tail tip, right?"

"How do you know that?" asked Dylan, suspicion creeping up on him.

"I am very observant. It comes with the job. Plus, I saw you tie up such a horse out front. In any case, rest assured your horse will be made just as comfortable as yourself."

"I doubt that, because I plan on getting very, very comfortable."

His room was at the back of the hotel away from the street, which made it quieter than most. The first thing Dylan did on entering was dump all his gear on the floor next to the bed sporting pristine fresh sheets. He turned to give Williams a tip, but the door was already closing.

Fine, he thought. *No tip for you, and no skin off my nose.*

Sitting on the edge of the beautifully inviting bed, he took off his boots and flexed his toes. God, just sitting on something soft was a divine pleasure, and something a lot of people took for granted. It was the kind of thing a person didn't miss until they didn't have it anymore.

Staying here for a day would definitely help balance things out, he thought as he let his eyes roam over the ornate wallpaper and combination dressing table and writing desk. Christ, the room even smelled nice. Lavender, if he wasn't mistaken. If Dylan closed his eyes he could envision himself sitting in a field of purple.

After getting his wind back, he crossed the room in his stockinged feet to look out the window. The white-tipped mountain range stood majestically in the distance, but he couldn't resist craning his neck and gazing up at the blue sky overhead.

Nope, no Winged Terror. He didn't know whether to feel relieved or disappointed. But he knew better than most that just because he didn't see something, it didn't mean it wasn't there. The stories sounded like pure invention. Crazy talk. But so did a two-headed snake and a bearded lady, both of which he'd set eyes upon at a travelling freakshow two summers ago.

There was a knock on the door.

Dylan instinctively reached for his Colt, then reminded himself where he was. He shouldn't be needing the Peacemaker here. Besides, if he had to choose a place to die he could think of a lot worse places.

Catching himself just in time, Dylan said, "Yup, come on in."

The door opened slowly, almost seductively. Dylan held his breath, half expecting to be greeted by the sight of a buxom, scantily clad blonde, perhaps another perk of the Gold Star package.

Instead, Von Williams poked his twitchy little balding head around and said, "Your bath is ready, sir. If you'd like to follow me."

Well, if he couldn't have a woman, Dylan thought, a hot bath was the next best thing.

He wasn't wrong.

An hour later, he was back in his room, lying on the pristine bed wrapped in cotton towels, freshly shaved and scrubbed cleaner than he had been at any point in the past eight months. He felt more than cleansed, he felt revitalized. Born again. The only thing that could possibly make the day any better would be a nap.

Dylan's eyes fluttered open and there was the inevitable moment of panic. Where the heck was he?

He'd dreamed he was staying at some luxury hotel, with a soft bed and fine sheets. Then his senses swam back into focus and he felt the same warm, snug blankets encasing him. It was no dream.

The light had long since faded. It was almost completely dark. How long had he been asleep? Three hours? Four?

God, who even cared? He didn't have to answer to anybody and his schedule for the rest of the evening was empty. He thought about Doctor Johnson's offer of a drink at the saloon, tossing the idea around in his mind like some kind of socialite with a lot of options.

Under normal circumstances, spending time with a sheriff when he didn't need to was asking for trouble. But he couldn't envision anything going wrong, and he would be a fool to spurn the chance to rub shoulders with a doctor and a lawman. Dylan never knew when he might need friends in high places, especially friends in high places who felt indebted to him. Besides that, he could do with letting his hair down a little and maybe sinking a few drinks. It had been a long time. Well, a few days.

He quickly got changed into his cleanest jeans and shirt, wondering whether the Gold Star package included laundry and making a mental note to find out sooner rather than later. Finally, he reached down to pick up his gun belt and paused. Would carrying that thing around send out the wrong signal? Everyone seemed so damn nice here.

Against his better judgement, he decided to leave the Peacemaker in the hotel, along with just about everything else.

He did, however, pack his twin-barreled Model 95 Remington Derringer into his right boot because, as everyone knew, it was better to have a gun and not need it than need a gun and not have one.

As far as he knew, there was only one saloon in Dudsville, so there was little chance of going to the wrong one. He was curious about what kind of establishment it was. Judging by what he'd seen so far, it wouldn't be the kind of place with sawdust on the floor to soak up the blood and spilled beer. At least, he hoped not.

He was right. At first glance it all seemed very civilized. The place had a pleasant, relaxed atmosphere. He'd attended more rowdy calf birthings. There was a table of card sharps in the corner, a couple of small huddles, and a bunch of fellas lined up along the bar, one or two of whom smiled or cocked their head in greeting as Dylan passed.

"Whisky with ice, er, please," he said to the sturdy-looking lady behind the bar.

As Dylan rummaged in his pocket for the money to pay for the drink, he felt a light tap on the shoulder and turned to see Doctor Johnson. "Let me get it. I'm a man who's always good on my promises."

"I can see that. Thanks again," Dylan said, putting his purse away. "I feel I'm always thanking you for something."

"So stop thanking me."

Both men laughed and clinked glasses. "So how's the Gold Star package?" the doctor asked with a knowing wink.

"I don't have the words to describe how wonderful it is," Dylan replied, still laughing. He almost thanked the doctor again out of habit, but stopped himself just in time.

"Let me introduce you to Sheriff Wade," the doctor said. "He does a pretty good job of keeping things in check around here."

Johnson moved aside to reveal a smartly dressed, short, rotund man with an impressive handlebar moustache smoking a thick cigar. There was a sheriff's badge pinned to his lapel. "Thank you for the wonderful introduction, Doc," the man said in a slightly wheezy, high-pitched voice. "But I doubt I am worthy of such praise. This town practically runs itself."

"I'm sure you're just being modest," Dylan weighed in. He wasn't above sucking up to authority figures when the situation called for it.

"So you're the famous Mr. Dylan?" Sheriff Wade wheezed, holding out a puffy hand to be shaken. "You've made quite a splash around here, what with all the saving children from rattlers."

"That's me, Sheriff. Though I am hardly famous. Just being a good citizen. Pleased to make your acquaintance. I hope that splash is the good kind of splash."

"A splash is a splash is a splash," the sheriff said cryptically. "The important thing is that a friend of Doc's is a friend of mine. We go back a long way, he and I. Longer than I care to remember."

It was just as well the sheriff had a friend who was a doctor, Dylan thought to himself. The man was a heart attack waiting to happen. Being the shortest in the group, he had to look up in order to conduct conversation and his head was permanently cocked to one side, giving the distinct impression he was questioning every word Dylan and the doctor said, which was probably a good habit for a sheriff to have.

Dylan took a deep swig of whisky and ice, enjoying the sudden explosion of heat in his gullet. Even the booze was good quality. Most establishments either made their own or got cheap counterfeit stuff with fake labels on the black market and then charged a premium for it. God bless America. The land of opportunity.

Dylan was beginning to feel a warmth inside, and it wasn't just the whisky. Everything felt right with the world. If things carried on like this, he would have a hard time leaving Dudsville.

He should have known things were going too well and couldn't continue in the same vein. Luck, or whatever he wanted to call it, was never a gentle gradient. It was more a sequence of glorious highs and crushing lows lacking any rhyme or reason. The trick was to recognize the good times when they came, because it could all change in an instant with a single event having the potential to send things south.

That event happened shortly after ten o'clock, according to the big grandfather clock in the corner of the saloon, when Sheriff Wade was regaling his audience with a tale about three bank-robbing brothers, each of whom grassed on the other two, leaving the sheriff with three guilty men with two damning witness statements against them apiece. Suddenly, there was a commotion at the other end of the room, near the doors.

Dylan reached for his Colt, only to be met with an empty space on his hip where his holster usually was. He suddenly felt very vulnerable without it.

Dylan, Doctor Johnson, and Sheriff Wade all craned their necks to try to see what was happening, the sheriff being forced to crane more than most on account of his being so short.

Near the front of the saloon a man was wailing with grief and shouting, "Help! That bastard! He took my Felicity. You have to help me get her back, please!"

As if on some signal, the small crowd of patrons opened up a path directly to Sheriff Wade, who stepped forward with a lot of authority for a man who had probably sank half a dozen glasses of whisky.

"Arthur? What the devil are you talking about?"

"Sheriff! You have to help me. She's gone. It took her!"

Now Dylan could see the source of the disturbance was a frail, elderly gent wearing an old, scuffed fedora and walking with a cane. His eyes were wide with terror and tears streamed down his creased, weather-beaten face. Every few shuffling paces he would stop and shake his fist at the air in rage.

When he reached the sheriff and Doctor Johnson, the old man slumped dramatically to his knees. For one uncomfortable moment, Dylan thought he was going to start begging. Instead, he rolled onto his back with his arms and legs outstretched. Under any other circumstances the sight might have been comical. A hush had fallen over the saloon, and every eye in the place was trained on the unfolding spectacle.

"Get me a wet towel!" Doctor Johnson barked at the barmaid. "This man is going into shock."

With some effort, Sheriff Wade knelt awkwardly beside the old man. "It's okay, Arthur. You're safe. Now tell us exactly what happened."

The old man was staring straight up, his eyes still wide. "We were out walking on Main Street, just a minute ago, Felicity and I. Then, the Winged Terror came from nowhere, snatched her up, and flew off toward the mountains with her still in its grip. She was gone before I had a chance to do anything. Why was I so slow?"

"Did it smell bad?" Doctor Johnson asked. It took Dylan a moment to work out why it was relevant, then he remembered it was part of the folklore that had built up around the Winged Terror. The Doc was trying to ascertain if they were dealing with the same creature or not.

The old man's eyes widened still further. "Smell bad? It smelled like the devil's asshole! Like the Horned One himself farted in my face. I can still smell it now. Worst of all were the thing's eyes. They glowed in the dark like fires. God, they were the eyes of a demon. Please, Sheriff, you have to get Felicity back!"

"Calm down, Arthur; we'll do our best."

"I know you will, because I'll be coming with you!"

"Arthur," Doctor Johnson said patiently, kneeling on the other side of the prone man and dabbing at his brow with the towel the barmaid had given him. "The shape you're in, you'd be more of a hindrance than a help. You can barely stand."

"I'm old, sprightly, and furious!"

"You can be all those things and stay right here," Sheriff Wade said, getting to his feet. "I'll gather up a little posse and go get Felicity back for you. How's that sound?"

"Sounds pretty fine, son. Please hurry! God knows what that beast'll be doing to her by now. My poor Felicity!"

"Right, you heard all that, so I won't waste time repeating it," Sheriff Wade said, addressing the entire room. "Doc, your skills may be needed, can I count on you?"

"Of course"

"Who else wants to join? We need to move fast so I'm looking for just one other good man, preferably someone who can shoot."

A murmur passed through the crowd, but there were no takers. Instead, all the men simply looked at the floor.

"You found him, Sheriff," Dylan heard himself say, then immediately regretted it. What had happened to this Felicity was tragic, but it wasn't any of his business, and only fools stuck their noses in problems that weren't theirs. It was asking for trouble. But his short time in Dudsville had set his personal ethics bar impossibly high, and he didn't want to let these people down. Besides, what else would he be doing tonight except sleeping in that beautiful soft bed?

"Good enough," Sheriff Wade said. "I notice you ain't packin' and we're gonna need something a bit more powerful than toothpicks and bad language, so let's go get our guns and meet back outside this place in five minutes?"

"Sounds like a plan," Doctor Johnson said.

Dylan was already walking. He exited the saloon, strode up the street, into the hotel, and used his key to open the door of his room.

Luckily, all his things were where he'd left them, including his guns. Wasting no time, he tied on his gun belt and instantly felt more secure. A quick inspection told him that almost all the cartridge loops were full and his Bowie knife and pouch were still attached.

Next, he unsheathed his Winchester model 1873 and gave it a quick once-over. It'd been a while since he'd had to use this baby, but he wouldn't be without it. Not tonight. While the Colt was more effective at close quarters, the rifle was better at range. Like when he had to shoot things out of the sky. This Winged Terror was one adversary he didn't want to get up close and personal with.

Finally, he rooted around in his saddle bags until he found some extra rifle cartridges and stuffed them into his pockets, making a mental note to buy a bigger pouch if he was ever lucky enough to visit another store.

Less than five minutes later, he was back outside the saloon. Sheriff Wade was already there, holding a double-barreled shotgun, its polished barrel glinting in the moonlight.

"Thought I'd sacrifice accuracy for power and bust out Old Faithful," the sheriff said, noticing Dylan's admirion. "This little beaut would bring down an elephant. Where's the doc?"

"Here he comes," Dylan said, catching sight of Doctor Johnson crossing the street. "And he's not alone."

"Can I come?" Little flame-haired Jerry asked, bounding over and looking excitedly from Sheriff Wade to Dylan and back again while brandishing his treasured varmint rifle.

"I already told him he couldn't," his father snapped. "He insisted on asking you himself, and promised to go home without complaint if you tell him to."

"It's just too dangerous, Jerry," Sheriff Wade said. "We don't know what we might meet out there, and if anything happened to you, your mom would string us all up by our testicles."

"Testicles?"

"Let's just say it wouldn't end well for any of us."

"You have to let me come. I have a plan!"

"Go on, tell us this big plan of yours," the sheriff said, rolling his eyes. "And hurry up about it. We have to get going. Felicity is out there somewhere."

"I can be bait," Jerry said, desperately. "We all know the Winged Terror likes kids. You grown-ups are hardly likely to draw him out. He'll see you and fly away. But if he sees me on my own, he might just have a try. You can hide nearby and ambush it. Plus, I'm an extra gun. Four is better than three."

"You're making a lot of sense," Sheriff Wade admitted, stroking his chin. "God dammit, let's put it to the vote. What d'ya think, Doc?"

"I think I'm stuck between a rock and a hard place. If I let him come, Melinda will have my guts for garters, especially if anything happens to him. But if I don't, I doubt this one'll ever forgive me. And even if I tell him to go home there's no guarantee he'll go. He'll probably follow us in the dark and fall into a ravine or something. I'd rather have him close by so I can keep an eye on him."

"What say you, Mr. Dylan?" the sheriff asked.

Dylan looked at Jerry's upturned face and couldn't help but see a little part of his young self. Jerry might be a kid, but he was strong and determined. Age or size shouldn't stop anybody doing anything. "I say let him come."

"Yes!" yelled Jerry excitedly.

"That's decided, then," the sheriff said. "We have to get going. There's gonna be a lot of walking involved, boy. Are you sure you're up to the challenge?"

"Yes, sir."

"Well, let's go and get Arthur his dog back."

"His dog?" said Dylan, confused. "I thought Felicity was his wife."

"Nope. Felicity is his Dachshund. He loves that mutt more than life itself."

"So we're all risking our lives for a dog?"

"Pretty much," agreed the sheriff.

"And for future victims," chipped in Doctor Johnson. "Not to mention all the ones in the past, if we're being public spirited."

"Well, let's just hope we don't run into any more rattlesnakes, eh Jerry?" Dylan said, catching his little friend's eye and winking. "Or a bear with a sore ear."

-V-

The group took the only road out of Dudsville and started walking west in the direction of the mountains, which now stood like sentinels in the inky darkness. They were spread out in a line of four, with Sheriff Wade on the far left, Doc Johnson next to him, and Jerry sandwiched between him and Dylan on the right flank.

"Would we be better off taking our horses?" Dylan asked hopefully. A gunfight he could handle, but walking endless miles through the night just to get to one would be a chore.

"I think we're best off going on foot," the sheriff replied. "We can move just as quickly at night and can go places the horses can't. It's a clear night, moon's out, so we don't need lanterns for a while. That freakish thing might not even know we're following."

"Do you think we have a chance of catching up with it?" Dylan wondered aloud.

"Truthfully?" said the sheriff. "Prob'ly not. Wouldn't have let the kid come if we did. If it moved across land we might have a chance of tracking it, but not when it spends most of its time in the damn sky. But we have to try, for old Arthur's sake. He'd do the same for any of us, if he could walk properly. Did you notice his walking stick?"

"I did."

"We had some trouble with cattle rustlers a few years back," the sheriff said. "Long story short, things turned nasty, guns were drawn, and he ended up taking a bullet that was meant for me. Blew his knee right out and he never walked right again. I feel like I owe him one."

"Well, we're here now," Dylan said. "Might as well have a look around. Do we have a plan?"

"Plan is to head to the mountains."

"You think that's where this thing lives?"

"Makes sense, don'cha think?" the sheriff continued. "Not many people go up there, with all the rough terrain, so it can more or less do what it likes undisturbed. Prob'ly lives mostly off small critters, but there are a couple of small towns scattered around the base of the mountain, just like Dudsville, should it ever feel like a helping of people meat."

"Or pet meat," Dylan added.

They walked mostly in silence for the next two hours, each of them trying to stay vigilant and alive to the possibility of attack from above while simultaneously looking for any sign that they were on the right track.

The night was unnaturally quiet and still, as if every creature in the immediate vicinity sensed danger, and the air was filled with the sweet scent of pine. The sheriff and Doctor Johnson had both brought oil lamps but used them sparingly, lighting them only when they wanted to examine something in more detail, or to light the way when met with an area of particularly impenetrable undergrowth.

"From above, the lamps'll light us all up like damned Christmas trees," Sheriff Wade explained at one point. "But without them we'll be liable to trip over something and break a limb, or fall down a hole never to be seen again. I figure we choose the lesser of two evils, especially now we have the boy in tow. Say, are you tired yet, young Jerry?"

"Tired?" Jerry replied. "No, sir! I could walk all night. Or until we find that monster. And I will. You just see if I don't."

"Well, I admire your guts," Sheriff Wade wheezed, sucking in huge, asthmatic lungfuls of air as he hobbled along with his lamp in one hand and his shotgun in the other.

The sheriff was clearly hoping Jerry would complain of being tired and give him the excuse he wanted to call off the search. If anyone was showing signs of tiredness it was him, and it came as no surprise to anybody when the sheriff announced a rest stop, placed the butt of his shotgun in the dirt, and leaned on the twin barrels.

"We can head on back to town if you feel we're chasing a lost cause," suggested Doctor Johnson.

"Don't be an oaf," the sheriff replied, indignantly . "It'll take longer to go back in the dark than it did to get here. And then we'd have to explain to Arthur and everyone else in Dudsville that we gave up. We haven't covered five miles yet."

"Even with the lanterns and the moonlight, it's too dark to see much of anything," Dylan offered.

"Right," the sheriff agreed. "We're headed into the darkest part of the night, and that'll make the going slower. But it can only get better after that."

"Pop! Sheriff! Mr. Dylan! Come here!" Jerry suddenly called out. When the three adults had stopped to rest and talk things over, he had pushed on a little way down the trail. "I think I...found something."

The trio cautiously approached the boy, guns at the ready and eyes scanning everywhere at once.

Jerry was standing over something near the edge of the path, his lips twisted in disgust and his own rifle pointing at the ground, indicating he didn't feel any imminent threat.

By the light of an oil lamp they could see it was the corpse of an animal. Or, more accurately, it was a collection of body parts, mostly stripped of flesh and skin to show the gleaming white bone beneath.

The parts were still moist and mostly free of flies, indicating a fresh kill.

"What the heck is that?" Dylan asked nobody in particular, feeling the whisky he'd drunk earlier roil in his stomach.

Doctor Johnson stooped beside the grisly mound and held his oil lamp over it. Then, to Dylan's horror, he reached in with his other hand and held something up.

It was a dog collar.

"I think it's Felicity. That poor girl."

"Jesus. Arthur is going to be pissed," Sheriff Wade said, shaking his head.

"It could be worse," Dylan said. "I know it's a tragedy and all, but I'd rather see a dead dog lying there than a dead person."

"Are you saying a dog's life is worth less than a human's?" Doctor Johnson retorted.

Dylan considered this for a moment, then said, "Well, that would depend on the human."

"Would you mind keeping ahold of that collar, Doc?" Sheriff Wade said. "At least the old fella will have something to bury. Maybe wipe it off before you give it to him, though."

"I guess I could do that," Doctor Johnson replied, grimacing as he took a white handkerchief out of his pocket and wrapped the collar in it. "At least we know we're on the right track."

"Was it ever in doubt?" the sheriff said.

"Whatever did this ate most of her," Doctor Johnson observed. "And spat out the bits it didn't like."

"Let's cut the crap," the sheriff said. "I think we all know what did it. That damned monstrosity."

"I hate to break up this important scientific inquest," Dylan interrupted. "But did it occur to any of you that there might be a very good reason for it leaving that carcass here in plain sight?"

"And what might that be?" Sheriff Wade asked.

"It could be a warning. To us."

"What do you mean?" Sheriff Wade asked, just as a cloud momentarily passed the moon, plunging his face into even deeper shadow.

"I mean, maybe this thing is smarter than we give it credit for. At least smart enough to know we're on its trail, and it left this carcass as a warning for us to leave it alone. It could have left it anywhere, but chose to leave it right where we would find it. What if we're not the ones doing the stalking?"

As the words left Dylan's mouth, the statement sounded equal parts improbable and ominous, but at the same time terrifyingly plausible. Judging by the lack of protestations coupled with the awkward, lingering silence, the other group members were in universal agreement.

Suddenly, something in the atmosphere around them changed. It was hardly perceptible, and nothing a man could define with words alone, but the fact that every member of the group started shifting and looking around anxiously spoke volumes. Dylan weas familiar with the expression "making your skin crawl." It felt like he he was walking through a cave full of spiderwebs. The only time he could remember feeling anything similar was as he was preparing to enter the depths of Silent Mine knowing he might never make it out.

Then there was the stench. The coppery smell of Felicity's spilled blood hung in the air. It was too soon for putrefaction to set in, but the smell only served to mask something else. Something musty, earthy and organic, not unlike the odor a skunk would give off. What was it old Arthur had said back in town?

"It smelled like the devil's asshole! Like the Horned One himself farted in my face."

He wasn't wrong. And what Dylan could smell now was just the leftovers, the remnants.

Unless...

Dylan heard a noise, the sound of air being displaced as something large and streamlined sliced through it, getting increasingly louder as it drew closer. He had just enough time to look up to see a dark shape filling the night sky directly above them like a black cloud in the shape of a giant bat, complete with tapered head and two enormous flapping wings. In the middle of the head, just like the stories said, were two glowing red orbs.

Its eyes.

Dylan yelled a warning and ducked, and at the same time heard screams from more than one of his companions. For a moment, the world was filled with panic and confusion, and the four pursuers scattered in all directions as survival instincts took over.

He crouched in an effort to protect himself, and immediately felt the impact of the creature hitting his back, the force knocking the wind out of him and sending him to the ground. Losing his grip on the Winchester, he rolled and reached for his Colt.

When Dylan levelled his weapon to fire, he saw the creature was now standing on the spot where the group had been just moments earlier. There was something deliberate about the action, as if the creature was trying to assert its dominance. That was when it fully dawned on him that as horrifying as they were, the stories were all true.

It stood at least eight feet tall, and had the arms of a human and the strong, bony legs of a bird, as well as a huge set of thick, leathery wings affixed to its back. The head, ears, and facial features were pointed and sleek, and the arms ended in taloned fingers, which it was using to grip Sheriff Wade. The man's face was ashen white and his eyes wide with horror as he was lifted off his feet while his mouth opened and closed wordlessly.

When the thing attacked, the group had lost both oil lamps. Dylan assumed Doctor Johnson had had the good sense to cover or extinguish one so the monster, because that was what it was, wouldn't be drawn to it like a giant moth to a naked flame. The other had shattered at the sheriff's feet and ignited the contents, the flickering flames now illuminating the terrible scene with a dreadful orange glow. Dylan was temporarily blinded by the sudden burst of light, so details were scarce. Later, he would be profoundly grateful for that small mercy.

There was a distance of about ten feet between Dylan's Colt and the target. The light was poor, he was in a prone position, and the creature was all over the sheriff. This could all go horribly wrong. He didn't want a murder charge hanging over him, so after cocking the hammer, Dylan took an extra few seconds to aim. He also had to deal with the pressure of knowing he had to take the shot quickly. This thing meant business, and a man's life was at stake.

Reluctant to try the head shot, he aimed instead for the creature's torso and slowly squeezed the trigger.

The unnatural stillness was immediately and irrevocably shattered, and a little lick of fire coming out of the barrel confirmed that a bullet was on its way.

It struck home with a solid thud, knocking the creature off balance.

However, it didn't drop.

In fact, the hit seemed to have very little effect on the creature, which still held Sheriff Wade in the air with one long, sinewy arm.

Dylan had seen both men and animals take a bullet and keep on doing what they were doing. It was as if the body sometimes needed time to process the fact that it had been shot before it began shutting down. Invariably, within a few seconds, the incapacitating pain hit and then the effects of the trauma kicked in.

But apparently not this time. The creature seemed completely unaffected by the .45 slug that had slammed into its midsection.

No matter, there were five more where that came from.

Gritting his teeth, Dylan fired again, twice, overcompensating slightly to ensure he didn't accidentally hit the sheriff. The first bullet might have strayed wide, but the second clipped the thing's shoulder, spinning it around. For some reason it had far more of an effect than the first shot, which had found the Winged Terror's torso, perhaps because that particular slug had hit an armored or otherwise protected area.

The creature dropped Sheriff Wade, who slumped to the ground gasping for air, then it turned to face Dylan, who still lay on his belly, and let out a blood-curdling roar that reverberated through the night like a foghorn.

For the first time, Dylan saw the thing's face in all its glory. The blazing red eyes were almost hypnotic, but they were also full of unmistakable intelligence. It went beyond the kind of sentient awareness displayed by Skydance and other trained animals. This was more refined and calculating, like looking into the eyes of a man who wanted him dead.

And it wasn't just that.

Instead of conventional features, the Winged Terror sported a proboscis in the middle of its face, similar to a beak. Below it was a black-rimmed mouth, filled with row upon row of sharp, pointed teeth. Dylan noted with horror that they were either discoloured or still stained with blood. The poor light made it difficult to tell.

The Winged Terror lived up to its name by taking a step in Dylan's direction, slowly unfurling its huge, leathery wings, and roaring once more. It was angry. Apparently, inhuman monsters disliked getting shot as much as people did.

Dylan would be lying if he said he wasn't utterly petrified, but in precarious, life-threatening situations it often came down to fight or flight, and there was nowhere to run. If he headed off into the darkness alone, he would be easy prey. Instead, he gritted his teeth and emptied his gun at the leering creature. But by the time the last bullet left the chamber, the creature was no longer in the same place. Dylan looked skyward, and was just in time to see a kite-like silhouette cross the moon.

As he rose to his knees and hurried to reload his gun, another volley of shots came from somewhere to his right. A loud bang, followed by a smaller pop.

Doc Johnson and Jerry?

Sure enough, looking dazed and bewildered, the doctor and his son emerged from the dense foliage off to the side of the natural trail they were on. Doctor

Johnson, armed with a breech-loading Springfield, was already reloading.

"You two took your sweet time," Dylan said, quickly locating his Winchester and snatching it up.

"We were hiding in the bushes," Jerry said furtively, scanning the skies above them. "I couldn't get a clear shot. Pop neither. We had to wait 'til it let go of the sheriff. And then everything happened so fast. It was here, I was lining him up, you shot it, and then it was gone. Poof!"

"I did hit it, right?"

"At least two or three times," Jerry confirmed.

Doctor Johnson was now tending to Sheriff Wade, who was slumped onto his side. Dylan approached, and instantly knew the prognosis wouldn't be good.

"He's losing blood," said the doctor. "Lots of it. It's hard to see where, but that thing's claws must have caused some puncture wounds."

"To hell with that," Sheriff Wade said, sitting up. "I'll be fine."

"Probably," the doctor agreed. "But only if we get you some proper medical attention."

"You're a doctor, fix me up!"

"It's not that simple, I'm afraid. I need supplies. Supplies that I don't have out here. Bandages, morphine, ointment. Something to plug the wounds."

"Apart from that, we need to worry about that thing coming back to finish the job," Dylan said, still looking skyward.

"He's right," the sheriff said. "Get me up. And boy, grab my shotgun for me."

Jerry did as he was asked while Dylan and Doctor Johnson helped Sheriff Wade to his feet. No sooner had they done so when the man's knees buckled and he almost went straight back down.

"We need some cover so he can rest and I can assess his wounds," Doctor Johnson said. "There's a distinct possibility he might bleed to death or go into shock."

"I haven't seen a building since we left Dudsville," Dylan replied, supporting the sheriff's weight with an arm. He was heavy, and the doc was right; he was in a bad way and getting weaker by the minute.

"I did," Jerry said. "When I was hidin' I think I spied a shack or somethin' a little ways up ahead."

"Was there anyone in it?" Doctor Johnson asked.

"I dunno, I can't see through walls, Pop," Jerry said, now struggling to carry three rifles as well as the one remaining oil lamp and the sheriff's shotgun in his arms.

"Guess not," the doctor said, helping Dylan yank Sheriff Wade along the track. "Well, we gotta try to get there regardless. Anywhere with a roof will give us enough time to regroup. Stomp out those flames, boy. And keep an eye on the sky. Let us know if you see anything."

"Will do, Pop!"

-VI-

With Jerry keeping watch and leading the way, Dylan and Doctor Johnson half-carried, half-dragged a groaning, wheezing Sheriff Wade until they came across a tiny, decrepit-looking one-story dwelling a little way up the hillside just off the track.

"There!" Dylan said, setting about his task with renewed vigor. "Let's get him inside."

The door to the crumbling building was hanging off the hinges, which was either a blessing or a curse. It made it easy to gain entry, but would make the place harder to defend. If they could walk right in, anyone or anything else could, too.

Dylan was first through the door, supporting the sheriff with his left hand and holding his Peacemaker in his right in case the shack held any nasty surprises.

By the look of it, the place had been abandoned for years, rather than weeks or months. Not only was it devoid of any life, but it was devoid of furniture, apart from a rickety wooden table. A tiny wood-burning stove was in the far corner and debris littered the floor. The one-room building was fitted with two windows, one facing south and the other north, the glass having long been smashed, assuming there had ever been any.

Dylan and Doctor Johnson laid the wounded sheriff down on the floor, propping him up against the wall, as Jerry laid his armful of guns on the wooden floor.

"Did you remember the lamp?" Doctor Johnson asked.

"Sure, Pop," the boy said. He had hung the lamp off his belt, and took his father's question as a signal to light it again.

When the soft yellow light flooded the room, the group saw the true extent of the cabin's neglect. Not only were the windows smashed and mold creeping over the walls, but part of the ceiling had fallen in and the floor was uneven, the wooden slats cracked and warped with little shoots and shrubs poking through. There was a pile of old clothes or dirty rags in one corner, and a row of broken cupboards against the wall, the surface of which presumably doubled as a worktop. The hovel smelled like damp and urine.

The first thing Doctor Johnson did was take off the sheriff's blood-soaked shirt to inspect his wounds more closely. The look on the doc's face, combined with the amount of blood leaking onto the floor, told Dylan all he needed to know.

"Jerry, take your rifle and stand guard at the north-facing window," he said, mainly to get the kid away from what was truly an awful scene. "If you see anything, yell."

Dylan then turned the wooden table on its side and positioned it in the doorway to act as an emergency barricade. No doubt the creature, whatever it was, would be strong enough to get through, but at least they'd see it coming. He nervously assessed the windows, hoping they were too small to allow entry.

The doc had made a compress out of strips of material torn from the sheriff's own shirt and started pushing it against his shoulder and neck. Nevertheless, the blood continued to seep out in rhythmic pulses. The man's whisker-strewn face was deathly white. "How's he doing, Doc?"

"Not so good," the doc replied. "Deep puncture wounds and lacerations to his chest, shoulders, and neck. The way he's bleedin' I'm inclined to believe there's a nicked artery in there somewhere. Could be bleeding internally, too. Can you hear me, Sheriff? Do you understand what I'm saying?"

The sheriff writhed, moaned, and gritted his teeth.

"It's going to be okay. We're going to fix you up."

"D..." Sheriff Wade spluttered and coughed, pink foam spilling out of his mouth and sticking to his whiskers.

"What is it, Sheriff?" Doctor Johnson said anxiously. "What do you need?"

"I need... I need to tell you you're a damned liar. You're a shitty human being, you hear me?" Sheriff Wade coughed again and winced, then continued his tirade. "And I don't even care if your little tearaway son hears me speaking evil of his old man. He may as well hear it from me as someone else."

"Calm down," Doctor Johnson said. "Don't get agitated. You're not thinking straight."

"I'm thinking straight enough to know that you're giving me a fat face full of l...lies right now. Not five seconds ago you as good as told everyone in the room I was done for. I was right here! I might not be sayin' a great deal because I'm stinging like a bastard and tryin' not to die. Now here you are telling me it's going to be okay and you're going to fix me up. You're a damn two-faced liar."

"Feel better?" Doctor Johnson asked.

"Why, yes I believe I do," Sheriff Wade said, letting out another ragged wheeze.

"You keep hold of that anger. You're gonna be needin' it."

"Doc? Will you do something for me?"

"Sure, Sheriff. Anything."

"Reach into my pocket and get me a cigar."

Seconds later, the sheriff was lying on his back, his head propped up on some of the dirty rags, puffing out clouds of potent gray smoke.

Dylan couldn't help but flash the stricken man an admiring grin. There was life in the old dog yet.

"I might fool you all and walk outta here on my own steam," the sheriff said between mouthfuls of smoke.

"You might very well do that just to prove a point, you stubborn old goat," Doc Johnson agreed. "But you wouldn't get very far in that condition. You'd hit the deck harder than a drunken sailor. And there you'll have to stay because you're too big for us to carry. Why didn't you stick with that diet I put you on?"

"I did!"

"You're supposed to stick to it every day, Sheriff. Not just on Mondays."

"Well screw you and all that fancy science claptrap, anyway. Look where it got me, damn charlatan."

"Need I remind you, Sheriff, that it wasn't fancy science that got you here. It was a monster straight out of a damn nightmare. You seem like a man of the world," the doctor continued, switching his gaze to Dylan. "Have you ever encountered anything like this before?"

"The thing that attacked him?" Dylan flicked through his mental catalogue of strange and varied memories. There were some hair-raising adventures and even a few unexplained mysteries. But nothing came close to matching this. "I'm still struggling with the fact that this dumb fairy tale I thought you crazy people dreamed up is apparently real," he replied.

"See! I told ya!" Jerry interjected from his position at the window. "I told you it was real. Now you can go off and tell all your fancy friends that!"

"I sure will, Jerry," Dylan replied to appease the boy, failing to mention that he didn't have any fancy friends. No doubt Jerry was having a tough night. Though not as tough as the sheriff's. Dylan was no doctor, but he didn't have to be to know the man was probably going to be dead by morning. Even if they somehow managed to figure out a way to get him back to Dudsville, he would bleed to death before they got there. Probably the best thing all round would be for him to see out his final hours here, where it was comparatively safe and comfortable. For the time being, at least.

Everyone in the room was aware of these cold facts. Probably even Jerry. It was the situation they were in, and they were all going to have to deal with it. It seemed Sheriff Wade's way of dealing with his predicament was to meet it with pure aggression, while Doctor Johnson seemed more accustomed to treating everything with a healthy dose of black humor and dry charm. Yet when you studied him more closely, Dylan could see this quick wit was tempered with an orderly, methodical edge. He used it as part of his armor, which was exactly what he would expect from a doctor.

Leaving the doc and the sheriff to entertain each other, Dylan took his Winchester and went to the opposite window. "See anything out there on your side, Jerry?"

"No, Mr. Dylan. I thought it had come back once but turned out to be a buzzard."

"Well, there's something."

"Maybe it gave up and went home?"

The way Jerry made that into a question rather than a statement suggested he didn't really believe it. But hope is important. Especially for kids. Because without hope, and a belief that no matter how bad things get, tomorrow can always be better, life just isn't worth the effort.

Outside, the pre-dawn landscape was crawling with shadows. Knowing the Winged Terror might come back and finish the job at any moment, every rustle of a bush and every cloud passing over the moon made Dylan's heart race. His mouth was dry, and he had to constantly wipe beads of sweat from his forehead.

The time passed agonizingly slowly, every second marked by the ominous ticking of the doctor's pocket watch. The sound was almost hypnotic, and all Dylan could think about was the soft, warm bed he had sacrificed to come along on this doomedmission.

Lost in thought, he began to ponder the sheer randomness of it all. If he hadn't decided on that detour to Blood Lake, life would have taken him off in a different direction and he wouldn't be in this deathtrap with a doctor holding onto a collar from a dead dog, a kid, a dying man, and some sort of flying creature that wanted them all dead. He was a big believer in fate, if only because he had to believe in something. There had to be a reason for things to happen, or else why would they?

Damn. He had to stay alert. It was easy to drift off and lose focus. It almost always happened after a gunfight, or after he got attacked by a giant flying creature. There was a rush, when all his senses became amplified, and then came the crash, making him tired and lethargic. It was like his body went into recovery mode until it could find its natural rhythm again.

Something moved outside.

Of course something moved, Dylan chided himself. They were out in the countryside. Things moved out here all the time. And a fair percentage of those things wanted to eat them.

There it was again.

Not twenty-five yards away, he thought he caught sight of a slender black shape darting from cover to cover. Or was it just a product of his overactive imagination?

Dylan was just about to call the doc over for a second opinion when a huge leering face with shining red eyes loomed up inches from his own, filling the window frame. He staggered backward in shock, almost dropping his rifle. Afterward he would remember that moment, of coming face to face with the thing of nightmares, and feeling his blood turn to ice in his veins. The face was elongated and beneath the hooked beak-like protrusion in the middle, it appeared to be smiling.

Most memorable of all was the stench of putrefaction and decay everyone talked about. They weren't wrong about that. It was evident even above the sheriff's cigar smoke.

"You ugly bastard!" Dylan yelled.

Later, he would ask himself why he said that of all things. It was definitely a low blow. Not one of the group was looking his best by that point. But Dylan had to say something, and that was as good as anything.

As he yelled again to the others, Dylan swung the Winchester around and fired twice. The shots echoed, the noise bouncing off the bare walls a dozen times or more and plumes of acrid smoke filling the confined space. By the time the gun smoke had cleared enough to see again, the Winged Terror was gone.

Before Dylan could fully recover, there was a shout from across the room. His head snapped around just in time to see both senior and junior Johnson unloading on something they saw through their window.

Dylan was about to go over to investigate, and maybe get another chance of putting some lead into this monstrosity, when something massive momentarily obscured the window on his side. Knowing it would be too late even as he pulled the trigger, Dylan did it anyway. This thing was beginning to piss him off.

More shots on the other side of the cabin. The loud crack of Doctor Johnson's Springfield closely followed by the smaller *pop* of Jerry's varmint rifle and then another of Doc's shots.

"Jerry, put that peashooter down and grab the sheriff's shotgun," Dylan instructed, knowing the sheriff was unable to contribute anything to this firefight.

The boy threw his rifle down on the floor and scrambled to pick up the double-barelled shotgun, struggling with the weight and sheer size of the weapon. Dylan watched him go back to the window, use the ledge to support the shotgun's weight like he'd been using it all his life. The next thing Dylan heard was a deafening *BOOM* as the weapon was discharged.

Dylan was glued to his side of the cabin, and his window. Something was telling him to stay put, and stay ready.

Moments later, it was back. This time Dylan used his Colt, as it was more suited to close quarters, and emptied it into the night, more out of hope than expectation. He'd had more than one shot at it from point blank range and had failed to put it down.

"Is that thing bulletproof?" Dylan yelled.

"I think it has some kind of armor, or more than likely the skin on its torso is too tough for bullets to penetrate," Doctor Johnson yelled back. "I guess it's a self-defense mechanism. Plus, it's a quick little scamp. There one moment, gone the next."

"It must be circling us. Like a cat playing with a mouse before it kills it."

"Or..." said the doctor while taking aim at something Dylan didn't see and firing another shot.

"Or what?"

"Or, God forbid, there's more than one of 'em."

There was a brief lull in the din and an uncertain hush fell over the group. Smoke swirled around the cabin. Someone coughed.

"Did we get it?" Jerry asked hopefully.

"I have no idea," his father replied. "What are you thinkin' over there, Mr. Dylan?"

"I'm wondering how intelligent it really is."

"Not too damn intelligent at all if he's messin' with a pissed-off old Irishman on his damn deathbed," Sheriff Wade growled from his position on the floor.

"More intelligent than your average animal, that's for sure," Doctor Johnson said. "It's like it has an agenda. A plan. Most animals would give in to their survival instinct and scram as soon as they had a chance. They wouldn't stick around and try to get even."

"Don't know about that," Dylan replied. "I heard of wolves out in Alaska. They ain't never seen a man before, so they have no fear. They just see you as food."

"I still can't help thinking this thing is toying with us," the doc said. "Why does it keep circling? Is it looking for our weak points, preparing to attack?"

"Maybe," Dylan said. "Or it might be duping us into wasting all our ammo."

"Which we been doing a pretty good job of so far."

"It must be scared of the guns, else it would just come through the door or window," Dylan said. "And if it's scared of guns, that would be because it knows guns can hurt it."

"Let's all take a quick inventory," Doctor Johnson suggested.

Dylan checked his pockets and his gun belt, then said, "Seven Winchester slugs and eleven for the Colt. Including what's in the chamber. You?"

"Ten."

"What about your sidearm?"

"I didn't bring one. I don't get into many gunfights in the office. I'm more in the business of cleaning up the mess they cause. I carry a Smith & Wesson in my bag if I travel. Just for protection. But I didn't bring my bag with me, either. I brought my Springfield instead. Jerry, how many varmint bullets do you have left?"

"Six."

"And Sheriff Wade, how many shells did you bring with you?"

"Wha?"

"Shotgun shells. How many did you bring?"

"Eight."

"Why did you only bring eight shells?" Jerry, of all people, looked disappointed.

"Look, kid," snarled the sheriff. "In case you hadn't noticed, I'm carrying a little bit of extra weight. I didn't want to be carrying a ton of cartridges around on top of it. Besides, I figure anything I can't kill with eight blasts of my little beaut just ain't going to die. The rest of the shells are in the pocket of my shirt if'n you want 'em."

With a grimace, Doctor Johnson unfolded the sheriff's blood-stained tunic, rooted through the pockets, located the cartridges and handed them to his son.

"Leave my Smith & Wesson in the holster where it belongs," the sheriff snarled. "I might not be able to use my double-barrel but I can sure as hell still use my six-shooter."

"No problem, Sheriff," Dylan replied. "You hold on to that."

"Let's use our ammo sparingly from here on in," Doctor Johnson suggested, not unwisely. "But it might not be a bad idea to squeeze the odd one off just so that thing knows we're still awake and ready for it."

"So what's the plan now?" Sheriff Wade said. "We can't stay here and let it starve us out."

"It's too dark to see, and we don't have the ammo to waste," Doctor Johnson replied. "That creature might be able to see in the dark, for all we know. That would explain those unusual eyes. It might be trying to draw us outside, and if we've used all our ammo by then, we would be sitting ducks. Maybe it won't be so bold in the daytime, so why don't we wait until morning? Let you rest up and a little bit. Then we can make a concerted effort to high-tail it back to Dudsville."

"Sounds good to me."

Just then, the sheriff emitted a low, deep growl. But the sound didn't come from his mouth. Moments later, the cabin was filled with a new putrid stench.

"Sheriff, did you just fart?" Dylan asked, already knowing the answer.

"Think I did more than fart," the sheriff replied after another wheezing cough. "Unless farts now have the capability to soak into the seat of your pants."

"You pooped yourself?" Jerry asked incredulously.

"Yes, kid. It might surprise you to know that most of us go out of this world the same way we come in: kickin,' screamin,' and poopin' ourselves."

"That's almost poetic," Dylan said. "At least it would be if it wasn't for that Godawful stink."

-VII-

At some point during the long, empty night, Dylan might have rested his head on his hands and dozed off for a few minutes. He was dimly aware of Doctor Johnson and Jerry taking turns at the opposite window while the sheriff made himself as comfortable as he could on the floor between them, the sound of his ragged, irregular breathing filling the ruined structure. There was a brief pre-dawn period when the stillness was at its baleful peak and reality seemed to flicker in and out as the countryside came to life. For a while, Dylan wasn't even sure if he was awake or asleep and dreaming.

There was no sign of the Winged Terror. Nothing definitive, anyway. Had it given up and left? Had one of them managed to hit it and bring it down somewhere unseen? Or was it still out there, watching them and biding its time?

On one occasion, Dylan's train of thought was rudely derailed by a loud boom. It was Doctor Johnson with his Springfield. Now, he was cursing and scrambling to reload the rifle while simultaneously trying to duck and peer through the window opening.

"Get it?" Dylan asked hopefully.

"Pretty sure I saw it. Whether I made that particular bullet count or not is a different story."

"Or it might've just been another buzzard, Pop," Jerry offered helpfully.

Having only spent a short time with the boy, Dylan could already see he was blessed with all the qualities that should take him far in life, chief among them practicality, guts, and a heavy helping of honesty, which often came at the expense of being tactful. Tact took time to develop.

"Well, at least it knows we're still here," Dylan said to try to save what was left of the doctor's pride. This was a stressful time, and anyone could be forgiven the odd stray bullet or momentary lapse of reason. There was no point discussing it after it was done. All they could do was accept the new set of circumstances and adapt. Adaptability was a very undervalued skill.

Shortly afterwards the sun began coming up, spilling golden light over the mountains to the east and beyond. "Anyone bring any eggs or bacon?"

"I have half a packet of broken crackers somewhere," Doctor Johnson said. "It's going to be like feeding the five thousand. I didn't think we'd be out here this long."

"None of us did," Dylan replied, rejecting the offer of a cracker. It was so insubstantial it would do nothing to placate his hunger and would probably only make him hungrier. Besides, there were others who needed the sustenance more. It wouldn't hurt him to skip a few meals. He could do with a drink, though. "We got any water left?"

"Gave the last of mine to the sheriff last night," the doc said. "I'm not sure how effective it is in replacing all the blood he lost, but at least he's getting fluids of some kind back inside him. You alright there, Sheriff?"

At the sound of his name, Sheriff Wade's eyes fluttered open. Until then he'd been lying flat on his back, motionless and white faced, so still that Dylan wasn't sure whether he had survived the night. "Lasting," he said, the words immediately giving way to a coughing fit.

Dylan couldn't fail to notice the streak of blood on the back of his hand after the man wiped his mouth. He'd been thinking. This deserted smallholding or whatever they were stranded in was in the middle of nowhere, miles away from both Dudsville and Blood Lake. He didn't know whether anyone had actually lived here at one time or whether some hunters had gotten together, built the cabin, then moved on.

It wasn't important. What was important was the fact that if anyone was planning on staying here for an extended length of time, they would need a water source. And that often meant a well. It couldn't be at the front or they would've noticed when they came in, and a glance through a gap in the makeshift barricade confirmed it. Nor could he see any tell-tale signs through either window. That left only the back.

"I'm going to have a look at something," Dylan announced, looking from Doctor Johnson to Jerry and back again. "I'm gonna need some cover, so one of you watch me from the door, and the other stay here and watch the windows. If you see any sign of the Winged Terror, shout out. Or, even better, shoot the bastard and save us all a whole heap of bother."

Without asking any questions, which indicated he was of the opinion that any plan was better than no plan, the doc nominated himself for door duty. As he and Dylan moved the wooden table away from the doorway, Jerry kept watch, eagerly hopping from one window to the other. He had a limited view, but could monitor areas that couldn't be seen from the back.

Peacemaker drawn and ducking to make himself a smaller target, Dylan squeezed through the opening. After a quick look up to make sure there was no giant bird thing loitering on what was left of the roof, he scooted around the tiny building.

Sure enough, whoever had taken the time to build the cabin had flattened an area out back and dug a well right where Dylan expected it to be. There was also a rope, hopefully attached to a bucket.

Yes!

Could his luck be hitting another upward curve?

Dylan jogged over to the well, scanning all around.

No monster.

Yet.

With some reluctance, he holstered his gun and used both hands to pull on the rope.

"Please, please..."

The bucket slowly came up, rebounding off the walls of the crude well on the way. He could hear water sloshing around inside, but was still half expecting the bucket to be full of body parts or severed heads, fate playing another cruel joke.

But when he dragged it to the rim of the well he saw it was only full of water. Cool, clear water.

Mission accomplished, Dylan unhooked the bucket from the rope and, gripping the handle tightly and being careful not to spill too much, worked his way around the cabin and back in through the entrance.

"Good work!" Doctor Johnson said, clapping Dylan on the shoulder. "That'll do us all a world of good."

They drank straight from the bucket, each man, and boy, thirstier than the last.

"Is the sheriff up for travelling?" Dylan asked. He didn't want to be the one to address the elephant in the room, but someone had to.

"Why don't you ask him yerself?" Sheriff Wade grumbled. "Sick and tired of people around here talking about me like I'm dead already."

"Last night was the big test," the doctor said. "And he passed it. Easy for a man his age to go into cardiac arrest. We managed to stem the bleeding, though that will no doubt start up again when we get moving, and we all got some of our strength back. But I do think it's time to call a halt to this mission and get back to Dudsville where we can regroup and I can treat these wounds properly."

"Seconded," Dylan said, before the sheriff could object. "That creature out there probably isn't going anywhere. If it's been here for centuries, it'll probably be here for centuries to come."

"Agreed," the doctor said. "We can come back another time with more men, more guns, and a better plan. Are we all in agreement, gentlemen?"

"I'm in agreement," Jerry said. He sounded relieved, and Dylan didn't blame him.

"Then it doesn't seem like I have a choice," the sheriff said, trying to struggle to his feet.

The entire left side of his body was drenched with blood. He had been leaking from his wounds throughout the night, and Dylan couldn't help but wonder how the man was still breathing. He must be as strong as an ox and as stubborn as a mule.

"Gather up our possessions," Doctor Johnson said to Jerry. "Leave behind anything we might not need. Any excess baggage will only slow us down. That includes the lantern and that varmint rifle of yours. You can't carry both that and the sheriff's shotgun. The varmint rifle isn't much good against whatever's out there, anyway. I'll get you a new one. Maybe a larger caliber. You deserve it."

"Wow, thanks, Pop!"

Sheriff Wade swayed from side to side, putting his hand on the nearest wall to steady himself. Then, purely on his own steam, he walked out of the door. The moment the cool morning air struck his face, he breathed in a huge, deep lungful. He probably wouldn't admit it, but he must have thought that was something he would never get to do again.

Doctor Johnson placed his hand on the sheriff's back to guide him. Dylan emerged next, Winchester at the ready, and the last person to leave the sanctuary of the tiny, crumbling dwelling was Jerry.

Dylan was still wary, but he, like the others, was momentarily preoccupied with getting moving again. It seemed like a long way back to Dudsville.

He knew something was wrong the moment he set foot outside. His sixth sense started firing, and later he thought he might have caught a whiff of that awful, sickly scent the thing carried.

But before any of them knew what was happening, the Winged Terror was on them.

It seemed to drop right into the group from a height, but not a great height, which suggested the creature had been standing on the roof. How long it had been there watching, listening, waiting, nobody knew.

It threw back its head and roared, the deafening sound one of rage mixed with what sounded like euphoria, then began wildly thrashing its impossibly long, sinewy arms.

Dylan heard the lethal sharp claws whistle through the air, then felt them rip into his right cheek, the impact making it feel more like a punch.

He was too slow to react and took the full force of the blow. The world tilted at a sickening angle, he was propelled through the air and landed heavily on his side, stunned.

From his position on the ground, he saw Doctor Johnson on his rump a few feet away looking dazed. It was impossible to see whether he was injured, but he was out of commission for now.

There was no sign of Jerry, and Dylan hoped the boy had the good sense to get back inside the cabin the moment the creature appeared.

Sheriff Wade was the only man seemingly unaffected by this latest intrusion. Probably aware that it was already too late for him, he wasn't trying to get away or even protect himself, despite the Winged Terror being mere feet away. Instead, he puffed out his chest, squared his shoulders, and drew his gun.

"Sheriff! Are you crazy? Get down!" Dylan yelled.

"No chance of that," the sheriff drawled, wavering slightly on his feet as he aimed. "I been cowering away from this abomination my whole life, and it ends today."

With a defiant, wordless yell, the sheriff emptied his Smith & Wesson into the monster before him, pausing only long enough to absorb the recoil before pulling the trigger again.

The interloper stood its ground, unfurling its gigantic wings and wrapping them around itself like a protective shield. The bullets landed with heavy thuds, as if striking a tree, but didn't seem to have any meaningful effect.

When the hammer of the sheriff's gun struck an empty chamber, the Winged Terror lashed out at the wounded man.

Sheriff Wade was too slow to react, and took the full force of the thing's claws across his throat. His mouth opened and closed silently, reminding Dylan of a fish out of water as fresh blood cascaded down the sheriff's chest. There was a surprising amount still left, considering he had been bleeding all night.

Sheriff Wade sank to his knees, his life force spent, as the imposing creature loomed menacingly over him.

Suddenly there were two more blasts, both much louder than the sheriff's gun had been, and the creature simultaneously doubled over and was knocked off balance. It howled again, though this time the rage was replaced with an element of surprise, and even pain. These were shots it wasn't expecting.

Jerry was standing in the doorway of the cabin, the twin barrels of the shotgun still smoking. That boy could certainly pick his moments.

Dylan knew he had to capitalize. Quickly. The creature was down, possibly wounded, and not protecting itself. Feeling the sticky warmth of his own blood running down his cheek, he drew his Colt, rose to his knees to improve the angle, and pulled the trigger three times.

This time, he aimed for the head and at least one of the bullets found its target, which was evidenced by the way the creature's head jerked back and to the side. It was stunned, if not mortally wounded, and Dylan steadied himself for the kill shot, convinced that neither man nor beast could survive a .45 slug through the eye. He tried to block everything else out, concentrate on the shot, and started squeezing the trigger.

But before he could get the shot off, with all the dexterity of a grasshopper, the creature leaped to its feet. Dylan now saw that the thick, muscular legs and ankles were covered in gray scales and patches of coarse black fur. Like its fingers, the legs ended in tapered talons or claws, giving the overall impression of something part bird, part human, and part reptile.

And then it was gone, using its powerful legs to propel itself into the air where it spread its giant wings and soared.

Reluctant to miss the chance now that the creature was in his sights, Dylan took the shot anyway, and was joined by Jerry with the shotgun. When the boy pulled the trigger, the recoil was so strong it almost knocked him off his feet. Undeterred, he aimed again and fired the second shot, before cracking the gun and reloading as if he'd been using it all his life.

The creature began circling above them, as if contemplating another attack. Was it intelligent enough to know it was just out of range? Seeing his Winchester on the ground, Dylan snatched it up and took one, last optimistic shot. Then he paused to survey the carnage left in the creature's wake.

Sheriff Wade was definitely dead this time. He was lying on his back, eyes glazed, and throat slashed so deep he had almost been decapitated, the gruesome inner workings of his neck now fully exposed and glistening in the morning light. Dylan swallowed hard and looked away, allowing himself only the briefest moment of reflection.

Doctor Johnson was groggy and disoriented but unhurt, proving as much by scrambling back to his feet and belatedly discharging his Springfield into the sky as the target was reduced to a mere dot. "Damn it. That thing is too quick," he growled.

Realizing it was useless and the chance was gone, he turned his attention to the sheriff lying in a spreading pool of his own blood. "God, look what it did. That could have been any of us."

"Hopefully it's flying back to hell," Dylan said, simply. "But I think it might be back soon."

Then he noticed something on the ground, near the dead sheriff's feet: a small puddle of what looked like a thick, black, viscous liquid. There were splatters and splashes of the same substance all over the immediate area, hanging off tufts of grass in stringy globules.

"What's that?" asked the doctor, following Dylan's gaze.

"I'm no expert, but I think it's what passes for the thing's blood."

"So we got it?"

"Sure seems that way. And judging by the amount of icky stuff, it's hit pretty bad."

"Good. I hope it hurts. Sheriff Wade was a damned fine man."

Rifle in hand, and with an anxious glance skyward, Doctor Johnson joined his son and Dylan in standing over Sheriff Wade's body.

"We can't just leave him here," he said. "He'll be scavenged and picked clean within hours. That's no way for a man of his standing to end up. He should at least get a Christian burial so the people who knew him can pay their respects."

"Good call," Dylan said. "But he's dead weight. No pun intended. Even the three of us wouldn't be able to carry him back into town. It would be a challenge at the best of times, but with no equipment or supplies, and at risk of another attack, it would be suicide."

"True," Doctor Johnson admitted. "What a conundrum."

"Why don't you two go on back to Dudsville and get some help?"

"What about you, Mr. Dylan?" Jerry asked.

"That job doesn't need three people. You two can move quicker on your own. I'll get the body back in the cabin and make sure that thing doesn't come back for second helpings."

"Mr. Dylan," the doctor said, using the same tone as he would when talking to his son, "no offense, but I'm not falling for that. We both know the minute we turn our backs you're going to go off chasing the Winged Terror up into the mountains. You don't seem like the type to leave a job half finished. And you probably wouldn't come back. Four of us couldn't take that thing down with all our combined firepower. You'd have no chance alone."

"Maybe not earlier," Dylan replied. "But it's wounded now. We might not get a better opportunity to finish the job."

"I still don't fancy your odds," the Doc replied sternly. "In any case, common sense suggests we'd be better off sticking together."

"That logic hasn't helped us yet."

"Still alive, aren't we? Three out of four ain't bad."

"Okay," Dylan replied. "So what's the alternative?"

"We stash the sheriff's body in the cabin, catch up with that thing and kill it, then all three of head back to town together to a hero's welcome when the job is done. We can either pick up the sheriff when we are passing or send someone from town for him."

"Are you sure you wouldn't prefer to get Jerry home safe 'n' sound?"

"Hey, I'm fine!" protested the boy, flicking his gaze from his father to Dylan and back again. "Don't worry about me."

"Realistically, I really do think we'll be safer in a group," Doctor Johnson said. "In ones and twos, it will be able to pick us off more easily. The best chance Jerry has of getting home is with both of us by his side."

"Fair comment."

"So come on, help me move the sheriff inside. We can use that table to block the doorway. Might help keep the coyotes out. Jerry, keep your eyes open. If you see anything, blast it with that shotgun."

"Will do, Pop!"

-VIII-

At the cabin's door, Dylan, Doctor Johnson, and Jerry paused briefly to consider the enormity of the task ahead of them.

"It's not too late for you two to head on back to Dudsville," Dylan said. "Don't forget to come back with the cavalry."

"I believe we've already had this conversation," Doctor Johnson replied, displaying a steely air Dylan hadn't seen in the man before. "And the answer is still *no*. Now it's personal. I want to see that thing dead."

"Me too," Jerry chipped in.

"Up to you," Dylan said, wiping a trickle of blood from his cheek as he slung his Winchester over his shoulder and carefully stepped over another rancid puddle of black liquid. "Then we'd better get going."

Deciding they had long since lost the element of surprise, if they ever had it at all, the trio planned to approach the mountains via the main path, the equivalent of the front door. The idea was to stay in the open as much as the terrain allowed so they'd be able to see the Winged Terror coming, and hopefully stay alive long enough to finish off the wounded creature.

When the path allowed, they walked in a tight group three abreast with Jerry positioned between Dylan and his father. It was the only protection they could offer. That and the guns. Each of them constantly scanned their surroundings, paying special attention to the area above their heads.

A mile or so up the path, Dylan stopped. Doctor Johnson and Jerry both read the signal and did the same.

"What's up?" the doctor asked, putting his Springfield to his shoulder and sighting down the barrel.

"There's something up ahead. See it?"

"Nope," replied the doctor, anxiously looking up and down and from side to side.

"Right there in the middle of the track."

"I see it, Pop!" Jerry exclaimed. "Looks like doo-doo."

"Excrement? What's so unusual about that?"

"Let's take a look," Dylan said, as the trio moved off cautiously.

It was a large pile of dark brown scat, so fresh the sun hadn't yet dried it out. Delighted flies buzzed around in a frenzy, landing on it and taking off again. Dylan kicked at it with a boot to break it up, then knelt for a closer look.

If there had been anything in his stomach, he probably would have brought it back up when he saw the chunks of matted dog's hair and fragments of bone in the stool. Evidently, everything the monster couldn't properly digest simply passed through it.

Then there was the stench. It didn't smell like normal poop; this was more meaty and sharp, more like rotting flesh. Mixed in with the turds was more of that black, stringy stuff they'd first encountered back at the abandoned cabin. Creature blood.

"Was it left by our friend?" the doctor asked, wrinkling his nose in disgust.

"Almost certainly."

"So what's so interesting about it?"

"You can tell a lot about an animal by looking at what comes out of its behind," Dylan explained.

"Such as?"

"Well, this has dog fur in it."

"Marvellous," the doctor replied sarcastically. "At least it doesn't have any of us in it. What else does it tell you?"

"It tells me that thing is badly hurt. The scat is full of what passes for its blood. It already lost a lot back at the cabin. Nothing on God's green earth can keep losing blood at this rate and hope to live long."

"If it had any sense, it'd fly away and keep flying," the doctor said.

"That may be true," Dylan agreed. "But I'm beginning to think something is driving this thing."

"Something like what?"

"Something like revenge. We hurt it, so it sees us as a threat that needs to be eliminated."

Undeterred, the trio pushed on as the sun rose higher and higher until it was beating down on them, causing each member of the group to break out in rivulets of sweat. Dylan wrapped his neckerchief around his forehead to keep it from spilling into his eyes.

The winding trail they were following was now taking them on a mild incline, which appeared to be getting steadily steeper as it took them deeper into the mountains.

The farther away from Dudsville they travelled, the more exposed Dylan began to feel and the more exhausted he became. He was sure Doctor Johnson and Jerry were feeling it too. He could tell by the uncomfortable silence, the labored breathing, and the furtive, nervous looks. They were in enemy territory now. This was the domain of the Winged Terror.

"Doc?" Dylan asked at one point, more to break the silence in a bid to put them at ease than anything else. "Can I ask you something?"

"Go ahead."

"Why hasn't anyone from town gone after this thing before?"

"Who says they haven't?"

"Well, how did it go?"

"As you can see, that thing is still flying around, so not very well. I remember a lot of posses being rounded up over the years and heading up here. Some were well organized, others less so. They either came back empty handed and frustrated, or they didn't come back at all. About six or seven years back li'l Charlie Woodridge was snatched just outside town. Middle of the day, it was. His father rounded up half a dozen men right quick. They didn't even bother getting their rifles and shotguns, just headed out with what they carried. A couple weren't even armed with anything more than shovels. Five of those men were never seen again. Only one returned two days later, and he was...changed. He lived out his days in an asylum, and to my knowledge died without ever telling a soul what happened to his mates."

"Didn't anybody ask him?"

"Sure they did. A lot of people asked him. But he couldn't answer. Struck dumb with fear or shock, he was. He was almost catatonic. Even had to be spoon fed until his dying breath."

"Why didn't you tell me that charming little story before?" Dylan asked.

"I didn't think it would help our case any."

"You're probably right about that."

It wasn't long before the path they were on became as steep as a staircase. It also shrunk until it was barely wide enough for them to walk in single file, and in places was almost fully overgrown with thick, lush vegetation. The sweet scent of pine filled the air. In just a few more weeks, Dylan guessed this route would be completely impassable.

Not that it would matter if you could just fly right over it.

Soon, the trio stopped to rest. The sun was making their clothes stick to their skin with sweat. They hadn't seen another person, or even an animal or a bird, all morning. It was uncanny, almost as if every living creature in the vicinity had gone into hiding.

They had each filled their canteens back at the cabin, but now their water was running low and the lack of food, or any reasonable fuel, was beginning to take its toll.

"Does anyone have any more water?" Dylan asked hopefully, acutely aware that they would need to resupply sooner rather than later. It would be a terrible anticlimax if they had to call the mission on the basis of not bringing enough supplies. His muscles were already beginning to cramp up.

"We should've brought the sheriff's canteen," Doctor Johnson said. "I left it with him. I know he won't be needing it where he is, but I wasn't overjoyed about drinking from a dead man's cup, so to speak. I didn't want to tempt fate. God knows the odds are stacked against us as it is."

"Well, we're not very likely to find any kind of stream or standing water this high up. Water runs downhill, remember. So let's try to conserve what we have," Dylan said.

"Will do," said Jerry.

The boy looked as fresh and full of energy as he had when they'd started this little adventure, and

Dylan was suddenly envious. This was probably the most meaningful and exciting thing to ever happen to the kid. Something he would carry with him the rest of his life. Dylan just hoped it wouldn't all end in disaster. It wouldn't be too long before all that youthful vitality would be sucked out of the poor kid one way or another.

From their position high up on the side of the mountain, the group could look down and see the sunlight reflecting off the rippling surface of Blood Lake, which only made their thirst even more acute. The water looked so cool and inviting from a distance. They could also see the wood and brick oasis of Dudsville, and Dylan wondered if there was still a gunman in the clock tower. How they could use him right now.

Dylan took his time looking around, not just to gauge their position but also to scan for threats, and trusted the doc and Jerry were doing the same. Each of them knew there was too much at stake to allow them to let their guard down even for a moment. There was no sign of the Winged Terror, but the unnatural hush lingered, making Dylan think the creature couldn't be far away. It might even be watching them, waiting for the right moment to attack. The mere thought made the skin on the back of Dylan's neck crawl.

Or was it more than just a thought?

Was some latent survival skill buried deep in his subconscious sparking into life and sounding a warning?

His suspicions were confirmed when he caught a waft of something beneath the overbearing scent of pine. It was the same stench he'd smelled before. But being able to smell it didn't make the Winged Terror any easier to spot. The scent was already dissipating, being carried on the stiff breeze, and it was impossible to pinpoint the source. All Dylan knew was that the creature was close.

He opened his mouth to shout a warning to the others when he heard a scream from behind him. He spun around to see Doctor Johnson being propelled through the air, having been struck from behind by something enormous and powerful.

The creature was attacking again.

It was after Jerry.

The towering creature extended a powerful, taloned arm and reached for the boy. Then there was a pair of loud *BOOMS* as Jerry opened fire with the double-barrel, the force of the spreading bunch of pellets pushing the creature backward.

From the angle at which he was standing, Dylan had a clear shot and made the most of it, firing the Winchester several times in quick succession. Learning from the previous encounters, he changed his approach slightly and aimed for the thing's feet. The awful, three-toed demonic-looking appendages didn't appear to be guarded by armor. For the first time, he noted with horror that each ankle had a spur on the back, like a giant chicken. What kind of abomination were they dealing with?

The bullets hit home, tearing into its feet. A chunk of discolored flesh was blown off amid a foul black liquid spray, and the creature howled.

As Jerry fumbled in his pockets for the last two shells and Dylan cocked and lined up the Winchester for another shot, the creature took to the sky again. This time, however, because of its damaged legs and other wounds, it failed to get off the ground cleanly.

Instead, it made an awkward, lurching leap over Dylan's head to land behind him.

He ducked and spun around just as the creature landed, stumbled, and made off up the path, which veered sharply to the right. He fired, but the bullet missed, ricocheting harmlessly off a nearby rock.

Doctor Johnson was now on his knees, groaning and rubbing his head. There was a lump the size of a fist above his right eye, which was already turning a bright shade of purple.

"What happened?" asked the doctor, looking around startled.

"It was the Winged Terror, Pop!" Jerry answered excitedly. "It came at us again. Did it get you?"

"I don't think so," the doctor replied. "I guess I bumped my head, though."

"I'm going after it. Stay with your father!" Dylan yelled to Jerry as he started to give chase, sensing the Winged Terror was beginning to weaken and no longer had the stomach for a fight. If it was able to fly and make good its escape, it surely would. This could be their last chance.

Despite being wounded, the creature covered ground quickly. Much faster than Dylan was able to on foot. It had left the path and was making off up the steep mountainside, moving with a mixture of bounding leaps and loping strides, its huge, paper-like wings opening and closing to give it lift when necessary. It reminded Dylan of a moth after it had been whacked with a rolled-up newspaper.

Fleetingly, it occurred to him that it might be leading him away from the group deliberately. And what if there was more than one? If this thing had been sighted in the area for hundreds of years, and by the local Indian population hundreds of years before that, there might be a colony of them rather than a single specimen. He could be heading straight into a trap.

Dylan's feet suddenly failed to find purchase and slipped from under him. He slid backward a few feet, losing valuable ground. Out of sheer frustration, he pointed his rifle in the creature's general direction and pulled the trigger twice more, knowing that even if the shots were on target they would likely be absorbed by its protective wings.

And then he was up again, pulling out handfuls of grass as he propelled himself up the incline. There was a stitch in his side, sharp pains tearing through his calves, and he couldn't catch his breath. He wanted nothing better than to just stop and rest. Who cared if the Winged Terror escaped?

But he couldn't do that. He owed the town of Dudsville, he owed Doctor Johnson and Jerry, and he owed Sheriff Wade.

The ground flattened out slightly, allowing Dylan to pick up speed. However, the creature was able to do the same. Dylan was falling behind.

He was about to admit defeat when he saw the Winged Terror's destination. Eighty or a hundred yards away, the ground dropped off.

It was a cliff edge.

The moment he saw it, Dylan knew the creature's plan. Lacking the power to get off the ground, let alone perform its usual array of aerial tricks, the only way it could escape would be to jump off the mountain and use its giant wings to glide safely to the ground. Then it could find somewhere to lie up and heal, far away from its pursuers.

Dylan considered letting it go. Even if he caught up with the creature, what could he do? He was low on ammo, and the thing was practically impervious to bullets anyway. Between them, the group had managed to inflict wounds, but those were hardly debilitating. It probably still had the strength and wherewithal to slash Dylan to pieces without breaking a sweat.

But in all the years the Winged Terror had been terrorizing the area, he doubted anyone had come this close to killing it. It felt like a once-in-a-lifetime opportunity. And if he didn't take it, the Winged Terror would no doubt come back with a vengeance.

Dropping the Winchester, Dylan put every last ounce of effort into catching up with the creature, forcing himself through the pain barrier and grunting with every movement. Slowly, he began gaining ground.

The creature must have sensed as much, because midstride it turned its head to glance behind and gave a pained snort when it saw how close Dylan was, its fearsome red eyes still blazing.

The cliff edge was approaching quickly. Which was a good thing, because if Dylan had time to think about what he was about to do, he probably wouldn't have done it.

He caught up with the creature just as it reached the edge. Using his momentum, Dylan threw all his remaining energy into his leap and grasped wildly at the creature's trailing leg. He succeeded in wrapping his arms around it, and was then either flying or falling. He didn't know which.

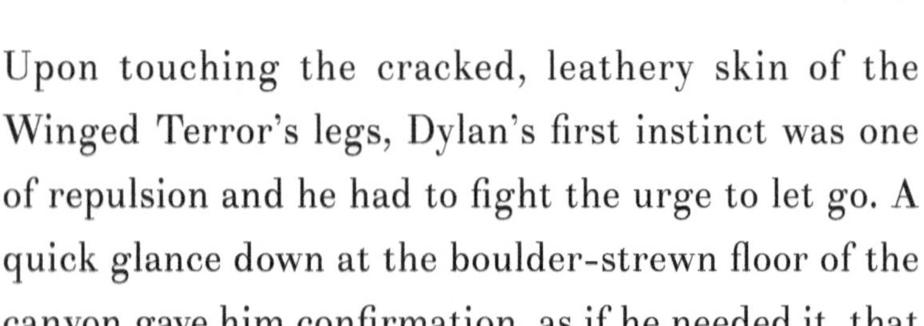

-IX-

Upon touching the cracked, leathery skin of the Winged Terror's legs, Dylan's first instinct was one of repulsion and he had to fight the urge to let go. A quick glance down at the boulder-strewn floor of the canyon gave him confirmation, as if he needed it, that letting go could only mean certain death.

Up close, the vile stench was almost overpowering, and the creature cawed and screeched like a frustrated seagull as it flapped its huge wings, gained some height, then went into a deep dive and kicked its powerful legs. It was trying to dislodge him.

Dylan gritted his teeth and clung on for all he was worth and only then, suspended far above the ground, did he begin to think about his next move. When he made the leap off the mountain his focus had been only on grabbing the creature to prevent its escape, hoping his weight alone would be enough to stop it getting airborne. It wasn't. He hadn't even considered that eventuality. Now, he was being forced to.

The Winged Terror kicked out again and executed a gravity-defying swoop. Dylan tried to take a breath, but the air was slamming into his face so hard he was unable to coax any of it into his lungs. Instead he closed his eyes, tightened his grip, and prayed for it all to be over.

Another swoop, and a lurch accompanied by those high-pitched, teeth-grinding howls. Dylan's stomach flipped over. If there'd been anything inside it, he was pretty sure it would have come back up.

When he opened his eyes again, he realized they were losing altitude. Fast. The creature's strength reserves must have been ebbing away, and carrying a passenger was affecting its ability to stay in the air.

It stopped flapping its enormous wings, held them out and started gliding instead, as if giving up on getting away and instead concentrating on controlling their descent.

It didn't work.

They were dropping out of the sky like a stone, picking up momentum with every foot.

Dylan started to think this was it for him. He had come as far as he could, and fought until the bitter end. His focus then shifted to ensuring that if this was to be his time, he was taking the Winged Terror with him. Using the last of his strength, he tightened his grip on its leg still further.

And then they hit the ground.

It didn't feel as if their descent had been slowed at all, but later Dylan would come to believe it must have, or else they would both be splattered on the rocks.

In the moments before the crash landing, Dylan tried to maneuver his body so the creature would take the brunt of the collision. He was partially successful, though his left arm got caught beneath them and his shoulder twisted awkwardly. He screamed as he felt the bone come out of its socket.

Even though he'd been expecting it, the force and magnitude of the impact both stunned and knocked the wind out of him. Most worrying of all, he heard something inside him snap like a twig.

Strangely, he felt no pain at first. Instead, there was a heavy numbness punctuated with white hot pins and needles. He could see them when he blinked, shining like stars in the night sky.

The Winged Terror gurgled and spluttered as if it were choking. Though Dylan had landed on top it, he had bounced off when they hit the ground and all he could feel beneath him now was the sun-baked canyon floor. Defying the pain in his shoulder and side, he raised his head to look at the creature.

It was lying on its back, and was even more horrific up close in broad daylight. Its tough, scaly skin was gray in color and its massive wings were spread wide. For the first time, Dylan registered the sheer size of them. They must measure a dozen feet across.

Its protruding beak was partially caved in, and more of that odious black fluid was leaking from its mouth and flaring nostrils as its chest rose and fell rhythmically.

It was still alive.

But only just.

"What are you?" Dylan growled, his voice a hoarse whisper. He couldn't catch his breath, and hoped to hell he hadn't punctured a lung. That would make his chances of walking out of here very slim indeed.

When he sat up, the pain flared, making him wince and groan. What did it take to kill this thing? With great effort he slowly drew his Colt, cocked it, and aimed.

And that's when the creature sprang to life, lashed out with a taloned appendage and knocked the gun right out of his hand. Whether it was playing possum or it had been knocked unconscious and suddenly woke up, Dylan didn't know. But he remembered the conversation he'd had with Doctor Johnson about the Winged Terror's intelligence level and knew that nothing was beyond the realm of possibility. It was certainly intelligent enough to know the gun could hurt it.

The sudden movement sent shards of pain radiating from Dylan's injured arm and shoulder and quickly spreading through the rest of his body. He knew his only chance of survival was to get away, and the absurdity of the sudden role reversal wasn't lost on him.

However, to his horror, he found he couldn't move a muscle. His body was too broken and battered. He could barely sit up, let alone run away.

As if in slow motion, Dylan watched the creature generations of townsfolk had dubbed the Winged Terror rise until it towered over him. Neither human, nor animal, nor bird, it was like some kind of relic from the prehistoric age, or a monster straight out of a scary bedtime story. They locked eyes, the blazing red orbs boring deep into Dylan's soul. At that moment he felt as if the creature wasn't just looking at him, but looking *into* him.

Blinking several times to break the spell, Dylan tore his eyes away and glanced at his Colt lying on the ground. He quickly concluded that it was too far away to reach. He could try, but something told him that if he made a grab for it, it would be the last thing he ever did. On the other hand, if he didn't try, he would be finished anyway.

It was an impossible situation.

The only other weapons he had with him were the Double Derringer in his boot and the Bowie knife on his belt. The Derringer was a non-starter. It had come to his rescue before, but not this time. He would need to take his boot off to reach it, and even then it was loaded only with a couple of small-caliber bullets. The creature had already withstood much worse.

That left only the knife, which was on the opposite side of his belt. The side with the smashed bones. He had no chance of contorting his body enough to allow him to get to it quickly, let alone use it. It was like events were conspiring to screw him over, but Dylan had fought back from the brink before, and would continue to do so.

The creature threw back its head and let out one of its blood-curdling roars, making Dylan shrink before it as if it were some all-powerful deity.

Suddenly, the noise abruptly stopped, and at the same time the glowing red light in its left eye blinked out.

There was just enough time for Dylan to wonder what had just happened, and what it could mean.

Then he heard the belated rifle report come from somewhere high up behind him, the noise so loud it reverberated around the canyon, and he understood.

Doctor Johnson had his back, and had somehow pulled off a miracle shot with that Springfield of his.

The Winged Terror retreated, making a low keening in the back of its throat as it staggered backward on unsteady legs.

Dylan knew now was his chance.

Wincing at the pain that wracked his body, he dug deep within himself and found enough strength to struggle to his feet, simultaneously unsheathing his trusty Bowie knife.

Even incapacitated, the creature stood several feet taller than him, and Dylan had to thrust the knife at an upward trajectory. The point penetrated its skin just beneath the chin and despite the blade's sharpness, immediately met with resistance, forcing Dylan to stand on tiptoe and use his knees to thrust upward to generate momentum. The skin eventually yielded and split open, spilling torrents of vile black liquid all over Dylan's outstretched hand and wrist. To his disgust, he realized it was only lukewarm, like the blood of a freshly killed snake.

The Winged Terror gurgled and spluttered, its shoulders twitching and trembling as if it were losing control of its bodily functions. Then it crumpled to its knees with Dylan's Bowie knife embedded in its throat.

But it still wasn't dead.

Dylan knew this was the time to exercise caution. He had been caught out before. The problem he now faced was that the only weapon he had access to was currently out of commission. Grimacing, he gripped the slippery handle of the knife and yanked it free. It came away with a wet slurp.

Dylan found himself gazing at the creature's ruined face. One of the eyes still blazed red, but all that remained of the other was a jagged hole. The doc's bullet hadn't just damaged it, but annihilated it. That, combined with the existing injuries, the damage it sustained in the fall, and the knife wound to its throat, suggested that the creature formerly known as the Winged Terror was no longer of this earth. And maybe it never should have been.

Now, Dylan had to finish it.

Twisting his upper body painfully, he put the Bowie knife back in its sheath and quickly located his revolver. Holding his injured left arm tight to his body to try to minimize the pain, he shuffled over and stooped to pick it up. Still wary, he didn't take his eyes off the stricken creature for an instant, right up until the moment his fingers brushed against cold gun metal. At that point, he wanted to get the job done as quickly as possible and glanced down just long enough to see where the trigger guard was in relation to his hand.

And that was when the creature struck.

Dylan could only think it had been silently watching him, biding its time. When that chance came, it took it.

As lithe as a cat, it rolled onto its side and lashed out with a taloned arm. Dylan felt an intense burning sensation on his shin and his world tilted harshly to one side as his legs were swept out from under him. The next thing he knew, he was on the ground again and the Winged Terror was scrambling all over him, dousing him with black blood as it reached for his throat.

Dylan couldn't reach his gun nor his knife, and the pain in his arm, shoulder, and entire left side was excruciating. His mouth, nostrils, and throat were filled with a thick, musty stench not unlike rotten mushrooms and he was soon covered in vile liquid.

"Why won't you die?" Dylan gasped, pushing down on the creature's meaty shoulders with his one good hand as he tried to extricate himself. Its massive set of leathery wings twitched and trembled, making him think that they would open and envelope him, crushing his bones and suffocating him.

Where was Doctor Johnson when Dylan needed him?

He was probably on his way down here with Jerry. All Dylan had to do was survive until they arrived. The badly wounded creature would surely be no match for the three of them.

But Dylan was used to being alone and solving his own problems, having learned and accepted that he couldn't go through life depending on other people. He could never completely understand their motivations, and there were always factors beyond his control. In any relationship there were too many moving parts, and too many things he couldn't know.

Instinctively, Dylan turned onto his side and stopped pushing down on the creature's head, using his hips instead to try to keep it at bay. His flailing hand closed around something cool and solid. He hoped it was his Colt, but he wasn't that lucky. It felt more like a rock, jagged and unforgiving.

It would have to do.

With a pained grunt, Dylan swung the rock. It smashed into the creature's temple with a thud, but seemed to have little effect. It was still coming for him, snarling, spitting, and dripping that tepid, black, mucus-like fluid.

He brought the rock down again, aiming for the same point. And again. On the verge of blacking out, Dylan clung to the vague idea that if he hit the same spot hard enough, or enough times, the thing's skull would eventually crack like an eggshell. Dylan closed his eyes and pounded away until he could no longer lift his arm, then he let it flop down at his side.

The creature had stopped moving. Instead, it lay motionless with its ragged, torn wings draped over its lower half like a funeral shroud. One side of its skull was caved in, white shards of bone plainly visible amid the glistening black and gray mush leaking onto the parched ground.

Fearing another trick, Dylan stayed still and listened for a few seconds. The only sounds to be heard were the thud of his heartbeat and his own labored breathing.

He might have passed out. It was difficult to tell. He came to his senses again when he heard voices nearby. Familiar voices.

"Mr. Dylan? Are you dead?"

It was a young voice, full of concern.

Jerry.

"I'm starting to feel like maybe being dead would be better," Dylan said through a rasping cough. "Get this thing off me."

Between them, Doctor Johnson and Jerry quickly pushed and pulled the slaughtered Winged Terror off Dylan, who was now not only battered, broken, and bruised, but covered head to toe in putrid creature blood.

"Phew. You smell bad," Jerry said when the job was done, wrinkling his nose.

"That's very kind of you to say," Dylan replied sarcastically.

"No problem," Jerry said, smiling and handing Dylan his Winchester. "Here. I found it up on the mountain. Figured you dropped it."

"Thanks, kid."

Hunching over and holding his side, Dylan retrieved his Colt once more, cocked it, and fired two bullets into what was left of the creature's forehead.

"Why did you do that?" Doctor Johnson asked. "I think we can safely assume it's dead."

"Yeah, we've assumed that before," Dylan said, thrusting the revolver back into its holster. "Better to be safe than sorry."

"Do you think there's any more of them out here?" It was Jerry who articulated the question they were all thinking.

"I'm inclined to think so," Doctor Johnson said. "There's no way for a single animal to procreate, so my guess is there's a small colony of them out here in the wilderness and maybe elsewhere. Who knows? Maybe they are all the same, or perhaps this one went rogue and turned to terrorizing people."

"Well, this particular specimen won't be giving you any more problems," Dylan said with a last, lingering look at the carcass. "Now I s'pose we'd better get the heck outta here before any more turn up. I don't have the strength, the inclination, or the ammo to fight another one."

"Good call," the doctor said. "Just by looking at you I can see you've probably sprung that shoulder and broken a bone or two. Maybe busted a couple of ribs. Let's get you back to the surgery and I'll fix you up. I'm sure Von Williams will let you stay at his place until you're fit enough to leave, and I reckon after what you did today, the townsfolk'll be happy to pick up the bill."

"That's very kind of you."

The trio turned, and started making their way back toward Dudsville.

THANK YOU

Thank you for reading *Blood Lake* by C.M. Saunders.

If you enjoyed this book, please leave a review on Amazon and/or Goodreads.

Amazon:
www.amazon.com/dp/B0FDY41B7S

Goodreads:

www.goodreads.com/book/show/237206277-blood-l
ake

C.M. SAUNDERS

Chris Saunders (he/him), who writes fiction as C.M. Saunders, is a writer and editor from South Wales. He has worked extensively in the publishing industry, holding desk jobs ranging from staff writer to associate editor, and is currently employed at a trade magazine. His fiction has appeared in numerous magazines, ezines, and anthologies worldwide, including the Literary Hatchet, Crimson Streets, 34 Orchard, Phantasmagoria, and DOA volumes I and III, while his books have been both traditionally and independently published. He has released six volumes of short fiction and several novellas, the latest being Tethered on 13 Days Publishing. Blood Lake is the second Dylan Decker book, following Silent Mine.

Keep up to date by visiting his website or socials:

https://cmsaunders.wordpress.com/
@CMSaunders01
https://www.facebook.com/CMSaunders01/

If you are a fan of horror stories and tales,
you'll want to follow Undertaker Books.
We're bringing you stories to take to your grave.